Stories

MIDDLE

Jim Gavin

MEN

SIMON & SCHUSTER

NEW YORK LONDON TORONTO SYDNEY NEW DELHI

Simon & Schuster
1230 Avenue of the Americas
New York, NY 10020

First Simon & Schuster hardcover edition February 2013

SIMON & SCHUSTER and colophon are registered trademarks
of Simon & Schuster, Inc.

For information about special discounts for bulk purchases,
please contact Simon & Schuster Special Sales at
1-866-506-1949 or business@simonandschuster.com.

The Simon & Schuster Speakers Bureau can bring authors
to your live event. For more information or to book an event,
contact the Simon & Schuster Speakers Bureau at
1-866-248-3049 or visit our website at www.simonspeakers.com.

Designed by Akasha Archer

Manufactured in the United States of America

10 9 8 7 6 5 4 3 2 1

Library of Congress Cataloging-in-Publication Data
Gavin, Jim
Middle men : stories / Jim Gavin.
            p. cm.
1. Men—Fiction. 2. California, Southern—Fiction. I. Title.
PS3607.A9845M53   2012
813'.6—dc23   2011045956
ISBN 978-1-4516-4931-4
ISBN 978-1-4516-4936-9 (ebook)

In memory of Barbara Gavin

Every life is many days, day after day. We walk through ourselves, meeting robbers, ghosts, giants, old men, young men, wives, widows, brothers-in-love, but always meeting ourselves.

—James Joyce, *Ulysses*

Contents

MIDDLE MEN

Play the Man

The Romans had a hard time killing Polycarp of Smyrna. In the stadium, surrounded by bloodthirsty pagans, he heard a voice. "Be strong, Polycarp," the voice said, "and play the man." The good bishop smiled calmly at his persecutors. They tried to set him on fire, but his flesh would not be consumed. They pierced his heart with a sword, but a dove issued from his chest. The afternoon dragged on like that, miracle after miracle, until they finally cut off his balls, or fed him to the Sarlacc pit monster, or whatever. I'm not a theologian, so I don't know all the facts, but eventually Christian artisans painted those divine words, "Play the man," on the gym wall of St. Polycarp High School in Long Beach.

On the first day of summer practice, Coach Boyd gathered us at center circle. I was going to be a junior and had just transferred from Trinity Prep, a bigger and better Catholic school in Orange County. St. Polycarp had one-third the enrollment, and it was all boys. I didn't know anybody yet, but according to my racial calculus—seven white, four black, one Asian—I would go straight into the starting lineup. It was 1992. Our shorts were getting baggy and Magic had AIDS.

"This is Pat Linehan," said Coach Boyd, putting a hand on my shoulder. "We're lucky to have him."

Trinity had the best basketball program in the state; I expected everyone to be impressed by my pedigree, but nobody seemed to care. Coach Boyd pointed to the fading mural of St. Polycarp.

"That's sort of our motto," he told me. "'Play the man.'"

"Do you mean man-to-man defense?" said a tall white kid with bad acne and luxurious eyebrows.

"You know what I mean," said Coach Boyd.

"Because we play zone."

"I know we play zone, Tully. Don't start with me."

Earlier, when I first walked into the gym, one of the black kids, Greg Overton, told me that I looked just like Dustin Tully. He was right, except I also had braces, which should've come off a while ago, but my dad had lost his job, and our dental plan, and now I was stuck with them.

Coach Boyd was barefoot. I found this troubling. Authority figures usually wore shoes. At the time, with his thinning blond hair and mustache, he seemed like an old man, but he was probably in his early thirties. "Now, listen," said Coach Boyd. "This summer we'll be taking a journey together."

"You mean the tournament in Ventura?" said Tully.

"No," said Coach Boyd.

"So we're not going to Ventura?" said Tully.

"We *are* going to Ventura, but that's not the kind of journey I'm talking about. Just listen for a second."

"Do you mean a *spiritual* journey?" said Tully.

"Yeah, but if you say it like that, it sounds stupid."

"Since we play zone," said Tully, "maybe our motto should be 'Play the zone.'"

— 2 —

"Do you want to run?" said Coach Boyd. "Because we can run all day."

"Polycarp was schizophrenic," said Tully. "All the saints were."

"Baseline," said Coach Boyd, and we spent the next hour running suicides.

For extra money my dad used to ref summer league games. As a result, I was lucky enough to grow up in gyms all over Southern California. At halftime I'd run down to the court with a ball, showing off my handle, my range. Even then I was a vain little shit. I imagined the bleachers full of college scouts, but the bleachers were usually empty. Summer league was a languid affair. Players yawned in the layup lines as their coaches sipped Big Gulps. In 1983, when I was seven, my dad worked a tournament at Cal State Dominguez Hills. The first game of the afternoon featured Crenshaw High, the L.A. city league powerhouse. They had John Williams, *the* John Williams, seventeen and already a legend. He walked in the gym and instead of warming up, he took a nap on the bleachers. I could hear him snoring. My dad blew the whistle for tip-off and one of his teammates woke him up. He walked to center court, still rubbing sleep from his eyes. Early on he got the ball on the right wing, drifted lazily to the baseline, then spun back, hard, into traffic, splitting two defenders, and though he could've dunked, he chose, with impeccable taste, to finish with a reverse layup. The beatific vision—you catch a glimpse and spend your whole life chasing it. At my next YMCA game, I tried to skip warm-ups and take a nap, but my dad yanked me up and threw me back among the mortals.

When I got older, he used to drive me around Long Beach,

looking for pickup games. If he drove by a park and didn't see a sufficient number of black guys who'd kick my ass, he'd keep going. His strategy almost paid off, because in eighth grade, after playing well in an AAU tournament, I was approached by a shadowy recruiter from Trinity—a "friend of the school," he called himself—who said I would be a nice addition to the basketball program. My parents, wanting to vouchsafe my future, agreed to take on the higher tuition and longer commute. When I got to Trinity, the coaches described me as "heady" and "deceptively quick," both of which meant I was "white." Apparently, I was using my superior Western European intellect to cross over fools and get to the basket. Somehow this didn't transfer to the classroom. In ninth grade, I flunked algebra. A counselor suggested I might have a tragic condition called "math anxiety."

My brain was average and so was my body. The coaches who liked my game kept asking when I was going to "fill out." I was six-foot and scrawny, with a weird concave chest that was a major source of shame. After playing JV my sophomore year, starting about half our games, I expected to move up, but several transfers arrived from exotic places like Westchester and Fontana and they were all seriously filled out. One kid was featured in a *Sports Illustrated* article as the best fifteen-year-old in the nation. At some point, Ted Washburn, the varsity head coach, called me into his office. He was a big man, with jowls, and in his Nike tracksuit, he exuded the portly air of a Renaissance king. After zero small talk he advised me to transfer so I could get some playing time. I vowed to fight for my place. "I like you, Pat," he said. "But you don't have a place here."

• • •

Coach Boyd finally told us to get water. As we drank from the porcelain fountain, sucking its leaden bounty, he conferred privately with Tully and then called us back to center circle. "I don't want to be an asshole," he said. "I had plenty of asshole coaches and I don't want to be like that. All I ask for is your respect."

That's when I started to lose respect for Coach Boyd. I thought we'd go into drills, but instead we divided up for a scrimmage. Chris Pham, the starting point guard, wore Rec Specs. He couldn't go left and every time he tried to change direction, I ripped his ball. I got down low and barked in his face, the way I had been taught. My rabid defensive posture amused my new teammates; they all sat back in a listless zone, waiting for something to happen. Tully was the tallest guy on the team, but he liked to hang around the three-point line. Overton and another black kid, Devaughn Weaver, swatted me a couple times, but otherwise I carved up their zone, either finishing or passing to someone with bad hands and no imagination.

After practice Tully asked why I had transferred. Anticipating this question, I had prepared a lie. "I got in a fight with a coach," I said.

"Did he try and rape you or something?"

"No."

"So the sex was consensual?"

"Don't listen to him," said Overton, laughing and pushing Tully out of the way.

Weaver asked about some of Trinity's players, guys with big local reps who were going to Pac-10 schools. I lied again, saying that before I left, I was also getting recruited.

"Serious?" said Weaver.

— 5 —

"Nobody good," I said, with preening modesty. "Fresno State. UC Santa Barbara. Places like that."

"I'm going to Cypress Junior College," said Tully. "My stepmom went there, so I'm a legacy."

I quickly changed my shirt, hoping no one would notice my weird concave chest.

"What's wrong with your chest?" said Tully.

"Nothing," I said. "It's just like that."

Everyone was staring. Pham switched from Rec Specs to glasses.

"My cousin's got the same thing," said Weaver. "It's all pushed in."

"It looks like somebody dropped a bowling ball on your chest," said Tully.

More than humiliation, I felt stunned by the cold accuracy of his description. That's *exactly* what my chest looked like.

My mom was waiting for me in the gym parking lot. She worked the perfume counter at Montgomery Ward and she was still in her nice clothes. My three little brothers were in the back of the minivan. They spent their lives getting dragged to all my practices and games. My mom turned on KOST-FM and we all sat in silence, listening to Barry Manilow. Just before the Los Coyotes Diagonal, I heard thumping bass and saw Tully cruising alongside us in a burgundy Chevette. Overton was slumped in the passenger seat, with his leg out the window resting on the side mirror. They were both drinking forties. At a light they pulled up alongside us and put down their bottles. My mom turned and noticed them.

"Those guys are on your team," she said.

"I know."

"Well, say hi!"

I stared straight ahead.

"What's the matter with you?" She started waving and yelling out the window, as if her life depended on this minor social occasion. "Hey! I'm Pat's mom!"

"Hello, Mrs. Higginbottom!" said Tully.

"Linehan!" she said. "We're the Linehans!"

"I'll see you at the regatta, Mrs. Higginbottom!"

My mom looked at me. "What the hell is he talking about?"

The light changed and Tully accelerated past us. Before getting home, we stopped for gas. My mom believed that gas was somehow cheaper five dollars at a time, which meant we were always stopping for gas. I pumped while she stood next to me, smoking a Winston Gold and squinting into the four o'clock haze. She was still baffled by the Mrs. Higginbottom business.

"Was that little shit making fun of me?"

We lived in a leafy neighborhood near the Long Beach Airport. When we got home, my dad was up on a ladder in the driveway, putting a new net on the basket. He used to be an electrician, but ten years ago he started teaching at a vocational school. At first it was for extra money, but after a string of knee and back surgeries, most of them the result of his continued participation in a men's basketball league, he happily started teaching full-time. He worked with apprentice electricians, helping them get ready for their journeyman exams. Since the school closed in January, he had been looking for contract work, but new construction had slowed down and he was having a hard time "getting back in the game." My mom didn't think he was looking hard enough. They had frequent arguments on this point. As we came up the driveway, he climbed down the ladder on his bad knees, wincing in pain, to make my mom feel bad for being such a tyrant. She walked past him without saying a word.

"Good practice?" he said.

I nodded. We had a real father-son thing going. Before dinner, I worked on my ball-handling. On the back patio I had set up an old full-length mirror and I spent an hour in front of it, trying to shake my reflection. My mom called me inside and we ate Costco lasagna, a bottomless pit of goo that had lasted for three days. After dinner, my dad came outside with a beer and watched me shoot my requisite two hundred jumpers. Twenty years ago he had been a second-team all-league selection at Mayfair High School. Now, he finished his beer, dropped the can on the lawn, and signaled for the ball. After missing his bank shot, he picked up the empty can and walked back inside. My little brothers had to rebound for me—it was on their chore wheel. Everything in the Linehan household revolved around the development of my midrange game. Even after my exile from Trinity, we were all operating under the assumption that I would eventually fill out and earn a scholarship somewhere. My mom kept assuring me that I was a "late bloomer." When I finished my drills, I granted my brothers use of the ball and went inside to watch tape. In 1986, I recorded the Big East Tournament final between St. John's and Syracuse, and since then I had watched it approximately seven million times, studying Pearl Washington's exquisite crossover.

After everyone went to bed, I put on another tape, an illicit Cinemax movie I managed to record just before the cable company cut off our service. The story dealt with the tribulations of an heiress. Most of her personal conflicts were resolved in poorly lit drawing rooms, among hirsute Europeans. The nonpenetrative frolicking didn't serve as masturbation material because I didn't masturbate. Ever. I'd just sit there, piously erect, a disciplined connoisseur of nipple and thatch. Even by apostolic standards, my repression was freakishly quaint, but I also remember enjoying these long passages of dreamy adoration. I've since read of Gnostic heretics in Asia Minor who, in abhorrence of their own bodies, sought a higher form of pleasure through the practice of *coitus reservatus*. Maybe that's what I had going on. Whatever the case, it meant that I was fifteen and still having wet dreams. At night I would sneak into the backyard and bury my soiled boxers in the trash can.

Coach Boyd handed out our summer schedule. First we had our rinky-dink Catholic league, and then the big tournament in Ventura. With a note of apology in his voice, he told me that St. Polycarp was in the same round-robin bracket as Trinity Prep.

"Will that be weird for you, Pat?"

"No," I said, feeling my stomach drop.

"Their loss is our gain," said Coach Boyd. "That's the way I look at it."

Before he took over in the spring, Coach Boyd had been a substitute teacher at St. Polycarp, and a volunteer assistant coach. During that first week, he kept arriving late to practice. He blamed his Volkswagen Thing, which had a tricky ignition. "You have to get it just right," he told us, jiggling an imaginary key.

I expected him to install some sort of offense, but every day he just rolled the ball out. "This summer," he said, "I want you guys to play free." I didn't want freedom. I wanted guys to run their lanes. I wanted to come off a pick with a second and third option. We had several "Big Wallys"—my dad's term for big, clumsy white guys. Tully wasn't a Big Wally, but he was the laziest guy I ever played with. This killed me, because he was actually pretty good. Now and then he'd drop step and dunk on someone, but otherwise he rarely made it below the three-point line on either end. Coach Boyd yelled at him a few times, and made us all run for his sins, but it didn't make a difference. I dove for a loose ball once and Tully started clapping.

"You're a coach's dream, Higginbottom!"

Overton was just as useless. He had the curse of the two-footed jumper: he was a highlight reel in warm-ups, but could never gather himself enough to dunk in an actual game. His dad, an Air Force mechanic, lived in Victorville, the high desert. Overton hated going out there—he referred to it as "Tatooine"—and he once brought a tumbleweed to practice to symbolize the desolation of his weekend. His dad wanted him to join the Air Force, but after graduation Overton planned to get a job in Hollywood as "one of those guys who do lighting and shit." He and Tully usually got high before practice. I never used drugs because I didn't want to make the same mistake as Len Bias, throwing away my golden future for one night of partying.

Weaver was the only guy I liked playing with; he understood when to cut and he could glide past guys, but he was high-strung, and if he missed a layup, or did anything wrong, he would slap his head and scream at himself and sometimes burst into tears. I asked Overton what was wrong with Weaver. "He's a Jehovah's Witness," he said, as if that explained everything. Coach Boyd spent a lot of time with his arm around Weaver, telling him not to be so hard on himself.

Pham graciously conceded his starting point guard position. "I'd quit," he told me, "but basketball looks good on college apps."

I dreaded summer league, playing teams that actually ran sets. The Trinity game was in three weeks, but I was already having trouble eating and sleeping. I'd stay up late, imagining miracles. I would play the game of my life and Coach Washburn would beg me to come back to Trinity. But these visions would give way to the nightmare of getting destroyed, over and over, by guys who were actually getting recruited by Division I schools.

One day after practice I expressed my frustration with the offense. Coach Boyd didn't have an office, so we sat in the bleachers.

"In the spring I tried to put in a flex," he said, "but it got too confusing and I started yelling at the guys. I hate it when I get like that. Then we had the riots and there was no use having practice. I don't know about you, but I spent two days in front of the TV, watching the fires, and all that . . . I really don't think it was anger. It was *pain*. Do you know what I mean?"

"At Trinity we ran motion," I said. "It's just down screens."

"I'm not good with systems," said Coach Boyd. "That's why I left the Jesuits."

I was planning on taking the bus home, but Coach Boyd offered me a ride. For ten minutes I sat in the passenger seat while he wrestled with the ignition.

"Come on, baby. Come on, baby . . ." He said it like a prayer, with his eyes closed. Finally the key turned over and the engine coughed to life. "Beautiful!" He put a tape in the stereo. "Have you heard the Minutemen?"

"No," I said, as something crunchy and propulsive rattled the speakers. The singer wasn't singing, just talking.

"What kind of music do you like?" Coach Boyd asked.

"I don't know."

"I used to see these guys live," he said. "I sort of knew the drummer."

For the rest of the ride he talked about the Minutemen. Apparently their lead singer had been killed in a car accident. "I cried when I heard the news," admitted Coach Boyd, who seemed to care way more about music than basketball.

Later that week, on my sixteenth birthday, my mom dropped me off for a job interview at K-Mart.

"Tell them you can start today," she said.

The guy who did the hiring went to our parish. My mom said I was lucky to have these kinds of connections. After I nailed the interview, they gave me a red smock and sent me to the checkout aisles. The woman I shadowed on the register kept looking at me funny. I thought it was because I was having trouble counting back change, but then she said, "Are you Dustin Tully's little brother?"

"No."

"You look like a kid who works here."

Pretty soon Tully strolled past the registers, pushing an empty hand truck. He didn't even blink when he saw me.

"You got something in your teeth, Higginbottom."

"Stop calling me that."

"Don't let them fuck you on your breaks," he said, leaning in close. I could smell beer on his breath. "Take your second break consecutively with your lunch, so you get forty-five minutes. They'll tell you not to, but you can do it."

A couple hours later, on my way to the employee lounge, I

saw him standing in Electronics, leaning on his hand truck and watching TV. "How do you like it so far?" he said, following me. "Do you want to kill yourself yet?"

We passed the Layaway counter. The girl working it, Jessica Ortiz, had gone to my parish school. She was speaking Spanish to a guy who wanted to buy a kid's bike. She handed him the slip and took the bike, which would remain behind the counter, in Layaway limbo, until he *finished* paying his installments. It was an insane way to do business. In junior high, Jessica always sprayed her bangs into an adamantine bubble, but now she had her hair pulled back in a slick ponytail. She had beautiful brown eyes and I used to spend a lot of time not masturbating to her.

"Jessica!" said Tully.

"Fuck off," she said, and then looked at me. "Hey, Pat."

"Do you know this guy?" said Tully.

"Is this your first day?" she asked.

"Yeah. I'm on the registers."

"Have you two dated or something?" asked Tully, as I stood there, blushing like Galahad.

"*No*," she said.

"Did he break cherry on your cherry?"

"I broke it on your mother's dick, you fucking homo."

"Jessica, I think we need to have an adult conversation about the integrity of your hymen."

"Do you have any weed?" she said.

"Meet me on the loading dock in ten minutes."

I went to the lounge, where a television was the only source of light. Two middle-aged women sat at a table, sharing an ashtray and watching the evening news. The lock on the employee bathroom didn't work, so you had to hang a sign on the doorknob that read, "Occupied/Ocupado." Later, at the register, as I waited for a price check, a strobe light flashed and bells started ringing. At first I thought it was some epic Blue Light Special, but it turned out to be the fire alarm. The whole store evacuated. As the fire trucks arrived, I looked across the parking lot and saw Tully wheeling Jessica around on his hand truck.

Coach Boyd usually ended practice with an inspirational quote. He liked Buddha, Lao Tzu, Saint Francis, all the barefoot mysticism of yore. The day before our first game, he switched things up a little and handed us each an old paperback copy of *The Call of the Wild*. He wanted us to read it by the end of the summer and write an essay about what it meant to us.

"I read that in fourth grade," said Overton. "It's about overcoming adversity."

"Okay. Maybe you guys are ready for something a little more . . ." Coach Boyd folded his arms and took a deep breath. "I don't think the administration will be too happy about this, but have any of you heard of a book called *On the Road*?"

"I've read that," said Tully.

"No, you haven't," said Coach Boyd.

"I'm serious. I love that book. I love its beauty."

"You've actually read Jack Kerouac?"

"Who?"

Coach Boyd turned to the rest of us. "I'll give you guys a choice. You can read *The Call of the Wild* or *On the Road*, which you can probably get at the library. Actually, you can read any book that seems interesting to you. And don't worry about the essay. Just read *something*, okay? That's your assignment."

St. Polycarp had a van that could safely seat nine people, and the next day Coach Boyd used it to drive all thirteen of us to Bishop Osorio High School in Watts. We tightroped up the 110, avoiding the hood for as long as possible, but eventually we had to get off and make our way to Central Avenue. There was no shade anywhere. A phosphorescent haze hung over the streets, making the sky feel like a wall. We passed an abandoned shopping center. All the windows were boarded up and in the middle of the parking lot there was a burned-out Fotomat. We stopped at a light and a few black kids our age were standing on the corner in front of a liquor store. They didn't notice us until Overton opened a window and screamed:

"Nigger!"

This must've been planned in advance, because Overton and the other black guys on our team immediately ducked down, leaving the black guys on the corner staring at a van full of white supremacists. We all ducked, except Tully.

"I remember that kid," he said. "He played at Osorio last year."

"Don't point at them!" said Coach Boyd, hunching over the steering wheel. Overton was laughing his ass off.

"Hey, man!" said Tully, waving. "Remember me?"

I heard obscenities coming from the corner. A soda can hit the window.

"Come on, baby, Come on, baby . . ." Coach Boyd was trying to will the light to change. I kept my head down until we started moving.

Everyone on Bishop Osorio was black, except for one Samoan. I felt buoyed walking into their gym with our black guys, who, in turn, seemed embarrassed to be on a team that was predominantly white. In the layup lines, Overton and Weaver only talked to each other. The Big Wallys rebounded in deferential silence. It was about ninety degrees in the gym. Our mesh jerseys were soaked and we spent most of our time wiping dust from the bottom of our shoes. Before the tip, Coach Boyd gathered us together and we put our hands in a stack.

"Play the man!"

Early in the first half, I crossed over Bishop Osorio's point guard and all his teammates laughed at him. It didn't happen again, and for the rest of the game it was hell just bringing the ball up the court. The whole summer would go like that: flashes of glory overshadowed by long stretches of competence. In this game, Tully actually played hard, or harder than usual; every time he got a rebound, he'd swing his elbows and yell, "Get the fuck off me!" Whenever possible I got the ball to Weaver, who had his little baseline floater going all game. We lost by ten, but played better than I expected. I never came out of the game.

"I'm really proud of you guys," said Coach Boyd.

When we got back to Long Beach, he pulled into a Jack in the Box and announced that he was treating us to milkshakes. In the drive-through, he realized he didn't have enough money. "Keep making them," he told the guy at the window. "I'll be right back." He drove across the street to a bank. For a while we all watched as he hunched over the ATM, pushing buttons. Then he tried to go inside, but the bank was closed. He pressed his face against the glass door, trying to see if there was anyone still inside. After a while he came back out and got in the van, but instead of going to Jack in the Box, we drove back to St. Polycarp in silence.

K-Mart paid in cash. On Fridays, I went to the cashier window, showed my ID, and they handed me an envelope with three twenties, a ten, a five, two quarters, a dime, and three pennies. My mom took her royal fifth for groceries and tuition, and I set aside the rest for getting my braces off. I was ruled by vanity. Our neighbors across the street had a pool, and before work I would sneak into their backyard, get down on my stomach, and dip my face in the water. The chlorine, I had discovered, dried out my acne, making it seem less rosy and bulbous. On my breaks I walked by Layaway, hoping to find Jessica, alone, but Tully always seemed to be there, leaning on his hand truck. One afternoon they walked by the employee lounge and saw me reading *The Call of the Wild*.

"Don't take your breaks in here," said Tully. "It's a graveyard."

"One of the greeters slit his wrists in the bathroom," said Jessica. "Security had to smash the lock to get him out of there."

"Where am I supposed to go?"

I followed them out to the loading dock. There were some plastic chairs set up behind a stack of pallets. "You can read your little doggy book out here," said Tully, patting me on the head, and they walked away.

After we lost by thirty to St. Callistus of Gardena, my dad found Coach Boyd in the parking lot and got in his face.

"You don't have a fucking clue what you're doing," he said.

My mom grabbed him, apologized to Coach Boyd, and

guided my dad back to the minivan. She drove home. My dad sat in the back, bouncing my youngest brother on his knee. "They're pressing full court," he said, "and Pat's stranded out there."

"If you were worried about *Pat*," she said, "you wouldn't embarrass him in front of everybody."

"Who hired that fucking clown?"

"*Language*," my mom hissed.

The next day at practice Coach Boyd asked if my dad was "okay."

"He just thinks we should put in a press break," I said. "That's all."

"Are you sure?"

"Trinity presses," I said. "We need outlets, and we have to keep someone behind the ball. I know how to set it up . . ."

"If you ever need to talk, about *anything*," said Coach Boyd, with a hand on my shoulder, "I'm always here."

I suppose my best friend on the team was Weaver, but all we did was hang around the gym together, killing time between our afternoon practices and evening games. We'd shoot around for two hours straight and not say a word to each other. Most guys ate lunch at Overton's house, which was close to school. Weaver and I only went there once. Overton's grandma made us grilled cheese sandwiches and we watched *Return of the Jedi*. The tape was warped from so many viewings.

"Imagine Princess Leia taking Jabba's dick," said Tully. "I mean, just *imagine* it. Seriously. Use your imaginations."

"Is she the only human girl in the whole movie?" said Pham.

"No, there's an English lady," said Overton, his sleepy eyes fixed on the screen. "She tells the rebels what to do."

"What was Trinity like, Higginbottom? You probably got all kinds of crazy South County ass."

I shrugged rakishly. As soon as Overton's grandma went down for her nap, Tully produced a joint, and so Weaver and I, the squares, retreated to the gym. During a game of 21, I ripped a fingernail on his jersey and it started bleeding.

"You got some nasty nails," Weaver said. "You should get them done."

"What?"

He showed me his pristine cuticles. "I heard Michael Jordan gets manicures. So I started going with my mom."

"Is it expensive?"

A couple days later his mom drove us to a salon on PCH. On the way over she kept asking where my family went to church, and if we liked it.

"I guess."

"Well," she said, looking at me in the rearview mirror, "maybe we could have a conversation . . ."

"Don't," said Weaver.

"Don't *don't* me," said his mom, as we pulled into the strip mall. She turned around and smiled. "We can have a conversation, right . . . what's your name again?"

"Pat," I said.

She dropped us off and went to run errands. Weaver told me to go first. He sat down in the waiting area and flipped through a glossy fashion magazine. My manicurist was a short blond woman named Michelle. She wore tight jeans and her heels clicked on the linoleum floor. The second she touched my hand, I got an erection. She asked if I was a Michael Jordan fan, like Weaver.

"No," I said.

"What do you mean, *no?*" said Weaver from across the room.

"I like John Williams," I told Michelle, but she had already drifted out of the conversation.

"John Williams?" said Weaver.

"He played at Crenshaw," I said. "He took LSU to the Final Four."

"Wait, *John Williams*," said Weaver, putting down his magazine. "You mean the fat dude on the Clippers?"

"Yeah," I said, and Weaver started cracking up. Williams, as a pro, had been a total bust. After putting on a ton of weight, he became known around the league as John "Hot Plate" Williams. I thought of my other two favorite players—Len Bias, who had died of a cocaine overdose, and Pearl Washington, who had washed out of the NBA after two seasons. Why did I care more about these guys than Michael Jordan? My erection was gone.

While Weaver got his manicure, I looked through the glossies. All the fashion models looked rich and angry. I had brought ten dollars—two and a half hours at K-Mart—but when Weaver's mom got back, she said it was her treat and invited me to dinner. I worried that she might want to have a "conversation" about the intricacies of their faith, but I was also sick of lasagna. They lived in a duplex on the bottom edge of Signal Hill. Weaver's mom cooked hot links on a grill, tongs in one hand, cigarette in the other. At some point Weaver's little cousin came by, wanting to play *Madden*. Lance was about ten or eleven. "Show Pat your chest," said Weaver, poking his cousin.

Without hesitation, Lance peeled off his T-shirt and showed me his weird concave chest. He didn't believe I had the same thing, so I had to show him. Lance looked confused and upset. "My mama said it would go away."

"It will," I said, and until this moment, I actually believed it *would* go away; but as soon as I said it out loud, I realized it wouldn't. Lance was quiet all through dinner. Mrs. Weaver had to work a late shift at Kaiser, but before she left she called Weaver into the kitchen. I heard them arguing in hushed voices, and then Weaver came out, with tears in his eyes, and locked himself in his bedroom. I played *Madden* with Lance, who kept running up the score. I think he knew some kind of secret code, because all his players were suddenly twice as fast as mine. Later, I called my mom and she picked me up. Before I went out the front door, Weaver came out of his room and handed me a pamphlet about his church.

"You can come to services with us if you want," he said, without zeal. "But you don't have to."

When I got in the minivan, my mom saw the pamphlet and freaked out.

"Those people *act* nice," she said, "but they just want to get their hooks in you. They're worse than the goddamn Mormons."

The week before the Ventura tournament, we managed to win a couple games. Even though I played well, I kept having nightmares about Trinity. Their guys would run past me as my feet sank into the quicksand floor, and then I would wake up.

On Friday night, after closing out my register, thirty dollars short, I escorted Jessica to the bus stop. Because of the payday cash situation, K-Mart employees were always getting mugged in the parking lot, usually by disgruntled ex-employees. Our supervisors encouraged a "buddy system" when leaving the premises. As we walked down to Bellflower Boulevard, she asked me how things were going at St. Polycarp. I began telling her about all the colleges who were recruiting me, but then we passed the Cal Worthington Ford dealership.

"I want a Mustang," she said suddenly, more to herself than me. "Black with a big-ass woofer in the trunk. Once I save enough for a down payment, I'm gonna go see Cal."

Just as we got to the bus stop, Tully rolled up in his Chevette.

"There you are," he said to Jessica. He was wearing a blue blazer with a light blue turtleneck. Overton, in the passenger seat, was wearing an Air Force flight suit.

"Get in," Tully said. "We're going on TV."

"What the fuck?" she said, laughing.

"Wally George!" said Overton, slapping the side of the car. "Come on, Pat. You too."

My mom was on her way to pick me up, but now all I could see was Jessica's ass, bobbing in front of me as she climbed inside. I followed and Overton handed me a forty. Jessica seemed to know I wasn't going to drink it. She grabbed the bottle from me and started chugging.

"Damn," said Overton, nudging Tully. "You were right about her."

Wally George was the host of *Hot Seat*, a conservative talk show on the local UHF station. A tall, cadaverous Reaganite with a platinum-blond comb-over, he interviewed pornographers, pacifists, socialists, homosexuals, dopers, punks, rappers, minorities, and all manner of human scum. His audience consisted mainly of drunken high school kids from Orange County, who were less concerned with ideological purity than with getting on TV and doing the pantomime for cunnilingus. The exception, tonight, would be Chris Pham, who, as Overton explained, was going with the sincere intention of throwing shit at Wally's guest, a Vietnamese merchant in Garden Grove who had recently hung a Communist flag in the window of his donut shop. It made the local papers and Pham's family had helped organize a boycott of his business.

By the time we got to Anaheim, Jessica had finished another forty, and now she and Overton were drinking a jug of Sunny Delight spiked with gin. Pham was standing in line outside the studio with a bunch of family and friends. He handed us each a button with an American flag on it and, underneath, something written in Vietnamese.

"Thanks for coming," said Pham. "It means a lot to me."

"I'm already fucked up," said Overton.

The parking lot was full of giant trucks, your basic OC Panzer division. A linebacker descended from the majestic heights of his Toyota 4-Runner. He saw some of his bros getting out of another truck and they all started broing out. The linebacker looked at everyone in line and said, "Go home, you fucking gooks!"

Pham's crew started screaming at him and giving him the finger.

"This is America!" said the linebacker.

"You dumb fuck!" said Tully. "Those gooks are on your side!"

The linebacker and his bros stepped toward us.

"Shut up," said Overton, kicking Tully's leg. "They'll kill us."

I just stood there. I was everybody's favorite guy—the

passive sober observer. A couple security guards appeared. I thought they were going to break up the race riot, but instead they ushered everyone inside.

Wally George's set consisted of a desk, an American flag, a picture of the space shuttle, and an oil painting of John Wayne. Jessica walked to the top of the bleachers and puked. It was all foam. Next to her, a guy in a rainbow Afro wig turned away in disgust. "I need Gatorade," she said, tugging at my red smock, which I had forgotten to take off, and I promised to get her some. When I got down the bleachers, I saw Overton chatting up a ponytailed cameraman, who kept pushing him away. I ran across the street to the 7-Eleven, but by the time I got back, the studio door was locked and the security guys wouldn't let me in.

I found a pay phone and called home for a ride. When my mom got there, she grounded me for a month, a purely symbolic act, because, with the exception of tonight, I never went out. We stopped for gas. As I pumped, she stood next to me and lit up.

"I have a question for you," she said. "Can you please tell me why you've been drinking out of the Lowrys' pool? Carol keeps seeing you back there. What the hell is wrong with you?"

"I'm not *drinking* it," I said, and I had to explain my acne situation. I saw relief in her eyes. She extinguished her Winston in the squeegee bucket and threw the butt in the trash.

"We can't afford a dermatologist," she said. "Not right now."

The show aired at midnight. The donut shop owner was clearly insane but that didn't stop Wally George from denouncing him as an enemy of the American people. Every time he slapped his desk in exhortation, the camera turned to the audience. I couldn't see Jessica or Overton, but there was Pham, his face red from nonstop booing, and there was Tully, posing in his blazer and turtleneck. He had brought an old-fashioned pipe. As everyone around him jumped and screamed and made lewd gestures, he just stood there, taking imaginary puffs, in the plummy style of Thurston Howell III.

At evening mass on Sunday, the celebrant, Father Meyer, read with feeling from the final canto of the *Purgatorio*, and from there he transitioned smoothly into a thoughtful and witty analysis of Aquinas and his notion of Angelic Knowledge. Or maybe he just told us that abortion was bad. Either way, my mind was elsewhere. The next morning we were driving up to Ventura.

After mass we got Del Taco and watched *The Simpsons*. I stayed up late shooting baskets, until my mom opened the front door and yelled at me to go to bed.

At some point that night, Michelle, my manicurist, sat next to me on the bleachers at St. Polycarp. Several Big Wallys were running up and down the court, and then Wally George was there too. It was a convergence of Wallys. Eventually, Michelle touched my chest and I woke up. It was three o'clock in the morning. I peeled off my boxers and snuck out the back door. Before I got to the trash cans, I heard music, and noticed a light burning in our old storage shed. I took a step toward it and kicked an empty bottle. The light went off, but not before I caught a glimpse of my dad, holding a beer and sitting on a rusty folding chair. There was a tape player at his feet. In the darkness, I could still hear music.

"Pat?"

"Dad?"

I wanted to ask what he was doing out here at three o'clock in the morning, but I also didn't want to know. I think he felt the same about me. We were both caught. The less said about our depraved nocturnal errands, the better. Now I could make out the voice of Bonnie Raitt.

"Everything okay?" he said.

"Yeah."

Moonlight fell softly on my spunk-laden boxers. For a moment we were quiet. "I wanted to come see the tournament," he said, "but I found some work out of town. I might be gone for a little while."

"How long?" I said, but he changed the subject and asked about my last summer league game, and I stood there for about five minutes, giving him the play-by-play. He never mentioned the fact that I was wandering around the backyard naked, and I never mentioned the fact that he was squatting in a dark shed, listening to Bonnie Raitt.

The van broke down on the 101. Coach Boyd pulled onto the shoulder and walked to an emergency call box. I had never been this far north. California seemed to go on forever. The freeway was surrounded by farms and I could smell manure. When Coach Boyd got back, he opened the hood and stared idly at the engine. The Triple-A guy arrived and informed us that we were simply out of gas. "My bad, guys," said Coach Boyd, laughing. "I forgot the gauge is busted."

We had reserved two rooms at Motel 6. After we put our bags away, Coach Boyd led us down to the beach, only a couple blocks away. We walked through a sleepy neighborhood and then over some sand dunes. It was overcast and the shoreline was littered with driftwood and seaweed. In the distance I could see a giant hotel right on the beach. I figured Trinity was staying there. Coach Boyd told us to sit down and relax.

"This is a big tournament," he said. "And I know for some of you it probably feels like the most important thing in the world—"

"It's just summer league. Who gives a shit?"

"I know, Tully. But *some* guys might feel like their whole lives . . ." He squatted down and picked up a handful of sand. "Listen. What you have to understand is that in the big picture, none of this matters." He let the sand fall through his fingers. "That probably doesn't mean anything to you guys right now, but it will. Because here's what's going to happen. Someday you'll be on a beach somewhere . . ."

"We're on a beach right now," said Tully.

"I know, but I mean like a beach in Mexico or something."

"What about the beach in Long Beach?"

"I guess," said Coach Boyd, "but it's a pretty crummy beach."

"I've always wanted to go to Hawaii," said Pham.

"Me too!" said Coach Boyd. "And that's the point. Someday you'll be on a beach somewhere, a *beautiful* beach, in Hawaii or Mexico, and you'll be with your friends, or your girlfriend, or maybe you'll be there by yourself. Who knows? But either way, evening will come and you'll see the sun going down in the water, and you'll get it. You'll just *get* it."

At two o'clock we drove to a local junior college. In our first game, Weaver played out of his mind. He dropped thirty, but we still lost. Afterward, we came out of the locker room in time to see Trinity warming up. We had to play them the next day. I watched the mesmerizing spectacle of their pregame drills and felt my stomach drop. Ted Washburn stood at center circle, surrounded by a retinue of assistant coaches.

"Is that the guy who raped you?" said Tully.

"We can watch a little of this game," said Coach Boyd, "and then we'll hit Sizzler. How's *that* sound?"

Since Weaver gave me the pamphlet we had been avoiding each other, but now he sat next to me and asked about all the Trinity players. "I can run with them," he said, suddenly full of himself. "One of their coaches said so."

"Which one?"

"I don't know if he was a coach, but he said he helps out the program."

During warm-ups, all the Trinity players wore custom Nike T-shirts with a nickname printed over their number. Mark McCracken, Trinity's best long-distance shooter, was "AT&T." Jelani Curtis, the fifteen-year-old featured in *Sports Illustrated*, was "Money." Darren Hite, a wiry small forward, was "Skeletor." Tully commented on how incredibly lame all the nicknames were, until he saw Andy Fague, the biggest wiseass at Trinity, whose nickname was "Nickname."

"That's not bad," said Tully, and it was the only time I remember him complimenting someone.

The game tipped and we watched Jelani Curtis put on a show. He handled the ball, zipped passes, buried jumpers. There was an ease and confidence to his game, a kind of regal nonchalance that I would later understand as the defining trait of all the great players who've come out of SoCal, from John Williams to Paul Pierce.

"We're fucked," said Overton.

At Sizzler, Coach Boyd paid for three all-you-can eat buffet dinners and everybody took turns with the plates. The waitresses looked annoyed, but they didn't say anything. I couldn't eat. I kept looking up and seeing Trinity's press in front me. Back at the motel, we played cards for a couple hours, and then Coach Boyd suggested we all go to bed. He was sleeping down in the van. A few minutes after we turned out the lights, Tully and Overton shuffled out the door. I couldn't sleep, so I spent most of the night in the bathroom, trying to finish *The Call of the Wild*, but my mind kept drifting to the game. At dawn I went out on the landing and saw Tully and Overton passed out in lounge chairs by the pool. They spent the rest of the morning smoking out in the bathroom.

On our way to the game, I had trouble breathing. When we got to the gym, a few Trinity players came down from the bleachers to say hello and wish me luck. In the locker room, I kept lacing and relacing my high-tops. The buzzer sounded and everybody went out for warm-ups. I couldn't move. Coach Boyd asked what was wrong, but the words were stuck in my throat. "I think you're hyperventilating," he said. "I'll go find you a bag."

He came back with the whole team. By this time I was sobbing.

"Jesus Christ, Higginbottom. You're worse than Weaver."

"Fuck you," said Weaver, and everybody laughed because he never cursed. He grabbed a ball and walked out of the locker room.

"I couldn't find a bag," said Coach Boyd, putting a hand on my shoulder. "Just take it easy, okay? This is all part of . . . remember that thing I said on the beach?"

"I don't want to go out there," I said.

"Neither do I," said Tully. "Should I pull the fire alarm?"

"Come on, now," said Overton. "We can do this."

"Yeah, it'll be our one shining moment," said Tully.

"You're right," said Overton, rubbing his bloodshot eyes. "I'm fucking high."

"Hey," said Coach Boyd, in his sternest voice. "You guys really shouldn't be getting high before games."

I sat there for a while, with everyone waiting on me. Coach Boyd kept assuring me that he had "been there."

"Fuck it," said Tully. "I'm pulling the alarm."

"Might as well," said Pham.

"All I want is a nap," said Overton.

Coach Boyd looked at all of us. "Are you guys serious?"

Tully disappeared. The next thing I heard was the hammering of a fire bell, and we all evacuated the gym.

The game only got postponed for an hour—I ended up with six points and twelve turnovers and Jelani Curtis dunked twice on my head—but during that hour, in the parking lot, as Coach Boyd apologized to tournament officials, I felt a miraculous sense of relief, because I knew it was all over, my future. Later that night, while everyone went to Sizzler, I sat alone in the room, watching the local news. The plan was to relax and "collect" myself, as Coach Boyd suggested, and I guess that's what happened, because instead of thinking about basketball, I focused all my attention on the local news anchor, her lips and the curve of her neck. I felt something rising in me, a sense of life maybe, this life, here, in a motel by the sea, and just like that, my Gnostic phase was over. I jerked off three times in an hour. *Ad majorem Dei gloriam.*

Bermuda

I once chased a girl to Bermuda. Her name was Karen and we met ten years ago, by accident, shortly after she moved to Los Angeles. At the time I was twenty-three and living with too many friends in Echo Park. Our apartment resembled a Moorish castle. We were on the top floor, overlooking a courtyard that sparkled with empty beer cans. Ravens nested in the lemon tree and each morning I awoke in the shadow of a minaret. Plus we had cheap cable. My room was one-half of the living room and my mattress was a single, a mighty single, floating on a sea of thin brown carpet, among neat stacks of records and magazines. My rent, including utilities, was $180 a month. None of us were overly employed. I had a great part-time job doing deliveries for Meals on Wheels, which meant I got to drive around the city, listening to the radio and knocking on strange doors. The cripples were always stoned and paranoid, but some of the more chipper octogenarians invited me in and told me stories; some even gave me gifts, bizarre gifts, sad gifts, my favorite a dulcimer, hand-carved by an Armenian man who lived in a North Hollywood motel. He whistled strange melodies and had tufts of knotty gray hair in his ears. One day I knocked on his door and he didn't answer.

I asked the clerk where he went and the clerk said he had left a few days earlier, without paying his bill. This kind of thing happened all the time. People disappeared. There was nothing I could do but cross him off my list.

My verminous roommates included the Brothers Rincon, Javier and Gilbert, who chose to paint houses a couple times a week with their uncle, even though the trustees of Cal State Los Angeles had seen fit to confer on each of them a bachelor's degree in computer science. The New Economy was still new and the brothers contributed in their own way by destroying each other nightly in marathon games of *GoldenEye*. After two a.m., when I retired to my mattress behind the living room partition, aqueous shadows flickered on the ceiling above me and I fell asleep to the clicks and taps of their heroic thumbing. Nathan worked as a bellhop at the Chateau Marmont. He was better-looking than the rest of us and made good money on tips, which he spent entirely on himself. Mark, in contrast, was short and bald and extremely generous with his money. After a brief, dishonorable stint in the Navy, he returned to Los Angeles with crabs and a deeper understanding of commerce. He scalped Dodgers tickets, hung around pawnshops, and though he didn't really sell weed, he knew enough people who did that he somehow got himself administratively involved; also, in a kind of feudal arrangement, every tenant of the castle paid him ten bucks a month for the cable he had spliced from the apartment complex next door. Other people came and went, friends, girlfriends, friends who became girlfriends and the other way around, sleeping on the couch, playing Nintendo, listening to records, leaving dishes in the sink. The dishes. For a while I always did the dishes. If I asked my roommates to do the dishes, they accused me of being a martyr. Eventually I just let their dishes pile up, and they were happy with this arrangement. Their squalor was carefree and strategic. The water bong stains on the carpet, the broken torchères left mangled in the corner, the crumpled bags of Del Taco, all these things helped them appear frail, lovable, and human, when, in fact, they were members of a band. They owned expensive vintage gear—most of it acquired by Mark— and they called themselves the Map. I didn't think of them as artists, a distinction that belonged, in my mind, to musicians who lost themselves in the creation of sound, rather than in some gilded vision of what they might look like onstage. Nothing inspires obsession like a reclusive virtuoso—my heroes were Harry Nilsson and Arthur Lee—and nothing is more annoying than invoking such names in the face of struggling amateurs. The Map accused me of being a snob. "I know," I said, cross-legged on my single mattress, squirting Del Scorcho sauce on my quesadilla. The Map wanted to be entertainers, which is not a sin. Nathan could actually write a decent hook. They all worked hard and I marveled at their evolution. Just three years before, they were a righteous hard-core band, playing week-night shows at Jabberjaw and declaring in their lyrics a grim and lasting solidarity with revolutionary groups throughout the Americas. Eventually they mellowed out and learned to play their instruments. Weed and acid brought a new appreciation for melody and soon their set list consisted entirely of spacey love songs. Because I had no musical ability, or any other kind of ability, they let me load and unload their amps.

It was a happy time and I couldn't wait for it to end.

I knocked. Maria Recoba lived alone on a hillside in Los Feliz. It was an old Spanish Revival house. From the street it looked very grand and elegant, with bright stucco facades and arched windows, but the rosebushes along the brick walkway were dead, long dead, and piled on the front steps were several years' worth of new phone books. I knocked again. Usually, if someone wasn't home I would drop their meal off with a pre-assigned neighbor, but Maria was always at home. I was going to leave but then I heard a record playing, something classical on piano. This time I pounded on the door. The record stopped and a moment later the judas window in the front door opened. A stranger stared at me. She seemed young but I saw streaks of gray in the black hair that fell across her face. Her cheeks were red and glistening with sweat.

"I'm sorry," she said. "I didn't hear you."

"Where's Maria?"

"Maria's asleep."

"Are you a nurse or something?"

"No," she said. "I'm nobody."

I didn't know how to respond to this statement. She didn't say it offhand; she seemed to mean it. In Los Angeles this was a rare thing to confess.

"I'm just sort of here at the moment," she said, opening the front door.

"Do you know Maria?"

"She wants to sell her piano," she said. "I saw her ad in the *PennySaver*. That's why I'm here."

"You're buying her piano?"

I sounded skeptical. It was a beautiful old piano and this woman wore old navy-blue corduroys and a ragged white T-shirt. She was tall and athletic-looking, with broad shoulders and long bony fingers. Sweat dripped off the end of her nose and I could tell she wasn't wearing deodorant.

"No. It's an old Bösendorfer. I just wanted a chance to play it. That's all."

"I thought that was a record."

"You've got a bad ear," she said. "Maria's nuts. She said I could come by whenever I want to play."

I held up a disposable tin container full of meat loaf and macaroni. "Can you give her this when she wakes up?"

"Sure."

Footsteps echoed in the tiled hallway. Maria came into the vestibule, leaning on a cane. Because she couldn't walk up the stairs anymore, she now slept in one of the smaller first-floor bedrooms, on a single.

"You stopped. Why did you stop?" Maria saw me at the door. "Brian, come in! Have you met Karen?"

We shook hands. Her long bony fingers were rough with calluses.

"She plays the piano," said Maria.

Maria kept the curtains closed, even in July, and it was dark and stuffy inside. I followed her through the living room. Everything was covered in dust. On one wall there was a framed black-and-white photograph of Maria Recoba and her late husband, Gabriel. The photo, taken fifty years ago in Buenos Aires, captured the aristocratic bearing that was still noticeable in Maria, even when she was slicing her meat loaf with a plastic knife and watching game shows. She told me the first day I met her that she wanted to hurry up and die so she could be with Gabriel again. They didn't have any children. She wore the same dress every time I saw her. She was haunting her own house.

"Why are you selling your piano?" I asked her.

"For the money." She pointed to one of those tasseled

Victorian lamps that look like a jellyfish. "I'm selling that too. I'm selling everything. I'm making a donation to Blessed Sacrament and then I'm going to die."

"Are you selling the house?" I asked.

"I plan to die in this house," she said, turning for the kitchen. "Let's have lunch."

"I should get going," said Karen.

"No," said Maria.

There was nothing to eat but the meal I delivered and some apples that a neighbor had picked out of Maria's backyard. She ate all her meals at a little portable table in the kitchen. The dining room table, an ornately carved slab of oak, was buried under piles of laundry. We divided up the macaroni and meat loaf and drank tap water. Karen took an apple in her hands and snapped it cleanly in half. I had never seen anyone do that before. I was amazed. I wanted to open the curtains so I could see her face.

"I don't know anything about classical music," I said.

"I can only play a few things," said Karen. "I'm not some classical freak."

"Someone eat my spinach," said Maria.

"We should open the windows," I said.

She started to say something, but choked a little on her meat loaf. She held up her hand to indicate that she wasn't going to die at this particular moment. "Go play something, Karen."

"I should go home."

"Where do you live?" I asked.

"Play something," said Maria. "Just for a little while."

We followed her back into the living room and Karen sat down obediently on the dusty bench. She turned a page in the book and took a deep breath. She never stopped or made

BERMUDA

a mistake. It was such hard work playing the piano. I had no idea it was such hard work. Maria sat down on a couch and fell asleep almost immediately. Karen came to the end of a section; her head dropped, like she had just been given terrible news, and then, slowly, she lifted her hands off the keys. She turned and seemed surprised that anyone else was in the room.

"That was great," I said, and for some reason it sounded cloying and false, like I had already made up my mind to compliment her before she had played a single note.

"Is Maria always alone here?" she said, looking at the shriveled little woman snoring on the couch.

"Health aides come by a couple times a week to make sure she's not pissing herself. And she has friends from church."

"It's sad."

"She has it better than most. A lot of them end up in ratty hotels downtown."

She finally looked at me. "It's nice of you to come by."

"I get paid."

She got up from the piano. "I should go while I have the chance."

I felt bad just leaving Maria on the couch, but I didn't want to be there either. When the front door opened, she sleepily called out, "Tomorrow, Karen."

"Okay," she said, but I couldn't tell if she meant it.

I followed Karen down the walk. Her blue corduroys were so worn it looked like she had sat in powder. She said goodbye and started down the hill.

"Do you live nearby?" I asked.

"Eagle Rock," she said. "I took the bus."

I stood next to my delivery van and we looked at each other for a moment, and then a moment too long, and she kept walking.

— 37 —

I got in the van and played with the radio. Then I studied my delivery list, even though I knew it by heart. I could see her walking down the hill. She didn't carry a purse. She took long bounding strides and didn't seem to notice the view. It was hot and hazy and the buildings downtown were a ghostly outline. I wanted her to disappear around a corner, so it would be too late. I'd have an excuse for not doing what I wanted. And this is what I wanted: to offer her a ride and spend more time with her and then fuck her and marry her and listen to her play piano. I was twenty-three years old. I waited and she finally turned the corner. I felt sick. A few minutes later, as I drove down Vermont, I saw her at a bus stop, cracking her knuckles.

"Go back tomorrow," advised Javier, eating cereal from a Bundt cake bowl that had been left behind by the castle's previous tenants. The kitchen was small and toxic, but all meaningful conversations took place here. Gilbert, shorter and less effusive than his older brother, leaned against the counter, nodding solemnly. It was midnight and we were listening to "Blues Hotel" on KXLU. For the last hour we had been trying to snap apples in half. None of us were strong enough to do it.

"I had my chance," I said. "Now it would just be weird."

"Everything's always weird," Javier said, his chubby face serene in the twitching fluorescent light.

"She plays the piano like she's digging a ditch."

"Go back tomorrow."

"She has scratches all over her arms."

"She probably has cats," said Javier, with a dark note of apprehension.

Nathan was sitting on the couch with my dulcimer and

with a new girl whom he hadn't bothered to introduce. He never introduced us to the girls he brought around the castle; it was some insidious form of musician etiquette. He was growing out his sandy blond hair, shaggy on top and triggers on the side. Mod was back, again.

"Is she pretty?" he asked.

"Not as pretty as you," I said.

Nathan laughed, sort of. He always tried his best to seem self-deprecating, but he did it out of some dimly understood social obligation to be modest and likable, not because he actually considered himself an equal to the ghouls he lived with.

The girl looked at me. She had bangs and a thin paisley scarf tied around her neck. She was prettier than Karen, but I felt sorry for her. Her small, delicate hands seemed incapable of real work.

"I'm Brian," I said. "Did Nathan offer you anything to drink?"

Before she could answer, Nathan strummed the dulcimer, loudly and vindictively. It didn't matter. If history was a guide, a month from now this girl would still be hanging around with us, playing video games with the Brothers Rincon, going through my records, and generally conforming to the improvident mood of the household, and Nathan would come home with another girl and not introduce her.

"Are we going out?" Nathan wanted to know. It was Wednesday night.

We walked down to our local. Nathan left us immediately and sat down next to a Vulcan-like humanoid replete with black trousers and white belt. He was a somebody who knew everybody. Booking agents, promoters, label people. Nathan, to give him some credit, was always whoring himself on behalf of the band. In this area he had finesse and refinement, an almost preternatural understanding of who was who. Nathan's girl drifted over to the old photo booth and disappeared behind the curtain. For a long time Gilbert kept looking over to the booth, but he stayed on his stool, nursing his beer. She hid in there most of the night. Mark showed up and bought everyone drinks. Now and then he would take off for a couple days and come back with an unexplained infusion of cash. Javier told him about my exciting afternoon.

"I've always believed in love at first sight," said Mark, who had the dead eyes of a goat. He was a bass player.

"She's got gray hair," I said.

"All gray?"

"Just streaks," I said.

Nathan finally joined us and Mark bought another round. Gilbert made a little house out of matchbooks and then crushed it with his fist. For two hours I skillfully avoided buying anyone a drink. As we walked home I thought of the girls I had dated, relationships born of proximity and attrition, close friends becoming girlfriends. There was a glacial quality about this that I liked—the endings as slow and acquiescent as the beginnings—but tonight, for the first time, I had a feeling of pure and sudden discovery. I told Javier that I was going back tomorrow.

"Good," he said, flinging his arm around me. "Even if it's weird, it's just weird. That's all."

I worked every other day, so Maria was surprised to see me.

"Did Karen come by?"

"Not yet," she said, and invited me in.

I insisted on opening up some windows and she finally

relented. There was a knock, but when I opened the door, it was another delivery guy. He recognized me and gave me a suspicious look as I stood there in the vestibule. Like any nonprofit organization, our benevolent mission was sustained by a ruthless bureaucracy. There were rules and liabilities. In the past, some delivery drivers had taken advantage of their position, stealing things from kind and demented old folks, and so now, technically, only caseworkers were allowed to enter a residence. I walked with the driver back to his van, telling him exactly what was going on: there was a girl coming by and she played the piano.

The driver didn't say anything. I could tell he didn't believe me.

"Maria put me in her will," I said. "Now I just have to kill her."

He got in the van.

"That's a joke," I yelled, as he backed down the steep driveway.

Over lunch I asked Maria about life in Argentina. Mustaches, bandoliers, I wanted the whole hot-blooded story, but she just shrugged. That was the past and she was heading merrily in the opposite direction. We ended up watching *The Price Is Right*. A Marine corporal won the Showcase Showdown.

"Good for him," she said, clapping.

I got anxious waiting and looked for distractions. Since I had never been upstairs, I asked Maria if I could take a look. She walked with me to the foot of the staircase. Halfway up the stairs I turned and looked back. Maria, down below, seemed farther away than I'd expected.

"Tell me if you see him," she said.

"Who?" I said, and I got a sudden chill, realizing she meant her dead husband. "Don't say that! You'll give me a fucking heart attack!"

I apologized for the profanity, but Maria didn't seem to care.

I walked along the landing. The first room was Gabriel's office, still neat and orderly, with a bookcase full of hardcover mysteries. I ran my finger along the dusty slats of his rolltop desk. His window looked out on the backyard and the eucalyptus trees rising up from the hillside. Across the hall the master bedroom had a small balcony facing the street. I stepped out and looked around the neighborhood. Birds, trees, telephone wires.

She was walking up the hill.

The phone in the castle was disconnected, not because we couldn't afford to pay for it but because after two years of taking the responsibility of itemizing the bill, collecting the money, and sending the check, I gently asked my roommates if one of them could take over, just for a little a while, and when none of them volunteered, I announced that I would never do it again and they would all suffer in a hell of their own making.

During those first couple of weeks, if I wanted to call Karen and make plans for one of our chaste and meandering jaunts, I had to walk down to a liquor store on Sunset and use the pay phone. I miss those days, calling places, not people. I miss the hassle of getting in touch with someone. Karen worked nights at a veterinary clinic. She had the evening shift and then stayed the night, feeding the animals and cleaning their cages. She slept on a cot in the backroom. She made less than I did but didn't pay rent. This was her new life, and like her old life, it already seemed like a total failure.

Many years ago Karen Kovac, of New London, Connecticut,

had received a full scholarship to the Berklee College of Music in Boston. She finished the program but failed to distinguish herself in any way. She had spent most of her time goofing around in a ska band, playing keyboards. Her advisers thought she would make a great teacher, however, and they helped her get teaching jobs, private lessons that paid well, but she had no passion for it. She moved to New York and lived briefly and disastrously with her boyfriend, the guitarist in her old band. Eventually she moved back home to Connecticut and stayed. She still gave private lessons in the wealthier suburbs but she preferred manual labor. For a long time she worked for the county parks and forestry department, planting trees and clearing wreckage after storms. When her mom got sick, Karen quit her job and became one of those shadow people who dedicate their lives to the ghastly twilight of cancer. Her mom endured two years of brutal treatments, then died. Her father was old and, more often than not, drunk. She had lived at home the last three years, pretending to take care of him, but he was a strong, stubborn man, a retired machinist, who ate livers and kidneys and bathed once a week. He was content to spend the rest of his days drinking and watching TV. He didn't need her, and she realized she was just hiding from whatever was next in her life, so three months ago she had moved to California. She was thirty-three years old.

Karen talked about her past with a kind of miserable glee. At times the intimacy of her disclosures felt like an elaborate shield, a way of keeping me away from her—I thought of an octopus inking the water—but eventually she stopped talking about her past, and started seeing me, the person in front of her.

Our afternoons were spacious and full of light. Most of the time we just drove around, exploring the hillsides and the empty side streets. I told her about the castle, exotic tales of indolence and vice, but I avoided taking her there. Karen was draped in my royal flag; I had staked my claim and I didn't want to share her with my roommates, especially Nathan. Instead, we drove around the city, talking and listening to music. It bothered me that she never offered to chip in for gas, but I thought it would ruin the mood if I talked about money. Everything else was great. She had seen Hüsker Dü live and we were both obsessed with Lenny from *The Simpsons*. I remember these things being immensely important to me at the time. She had scars on her knees that I wanted to touch and she remembered little bits of conversation that most people would forget. I thought that was encouraging. Sometimes we hung out at Maria's house. We would bring beer and Karen would play for a couple hours, until Maria fell asleep, and then we would sit in her backyard, where it was cool in the shade of the eucalyptus trees. One day, as Karen walked along the edge of a stone planter like it was a balance beam, she asked me if I liked my job. She rarely asked me questions, and I always felt excited and full of appreciation when she did.

"I don't know how much longer I'll do it," I said. "Eventually I want to go back to school and make more money. I plan to lead a boring and respectable life."

"Doing what?"

"I'm not sure. Right now I own a lot of records."

"That's not really a career."

"I wish I could play music," I said. "Knowing a lot about something you can't do—it's like being a eunuch."

She told me that she had always loved animals and wanted to be a vet. She was excited when she got her new job—it seemed like a foot in the door—but now she was slowly realizing that it would never work out.

— 44 —

"I haven't taken a biology class since high school," she said. "I clean up cat poop for a living. I might as well try and become an astronaut."

All she knew how to do was play piano, and she was only good enough to teach it to rich kids.

"I love listening to you play," I said. "The stuff you play sounds like what it's supposed to sound like."

"I know," she said. "That's why I'm so fucked."

Karen came to Los Angeles thinking she would get her own place near the beach. She ended up on the east side, in a shabby but not entirely murderous neighborhood. She hated being there and she also hated going out. She had always felt uncomfortable in bars, the expression on her face too hostile to attract friendly people, but not hostile enough, apparently, to repel lunatics. Her first week here she went to see a show by herself at Al's Bar. Before the first band went on, a man with an Ace bandage wrapped around his head asked if she could drive him to Fresno. "ASAP," he said, tapping her shoulder. She declined and waited to see who he would ask next, but instead he walked straight out of the bar. She said this type of thing happened all the time. She imagined that whenever she left the house, an all-points bulletin was sent to every freak in the city, who went screaming after her with single-minded purpose. She hadn't gone out since. She worried that she had come three thousand miles just to become a recluse, again.

We started going to the beach every day. I always took the freeway to LAX and then drove down an empty road that curled around the back edges of the runways. There were sand dunes and wildflowers and silver jets roaring over our heads and when we got to the end we could see the ocean. It was nice arriving at the beach around four o'clock, with people clearing out and the evening swell rolling in. Karen was a strong swimmer and never got cold in the water. She didn't own a women's bathing suit. She wore a dark T-shirt and a pair of board shorts that I had lent her. Under the board shorts, she wore men's briefs. She always wore men's briefs, because she considered women's underwear to be frilly and absurd.

"Don't worry," she said, snapping the elastic band against her salty skin, "I don't have a cock."

Sometime in late July, after we had bodysurfed for a couple hours, I came in, exhausted, and waited for her on the strand. It was almost dark when she ran out of the water. She sat down beside me, shivering, and for a long time we watched seagulls poking around the lifeguard tower. Farther up the coast I could see lights crowning the palisades and I thought, now, now is the time to kiss this cockless woman.

"Can I kiss you?"

"Yes," she said, with a look of resignation that, for the next two months, would never quite leave her face.

Later, at Del Taco, we had the conversation wherein the two parties recount their version of the courtship. She had wanted me to kiss her the whole time. For some reason, this knowledge was more satisfying than the kiss itself.

"This isn't going to work," she said, dipping her quesadilla in Del Scorcho sauce. "I hope you understand that."

A few nights later we had seedy proletarian sex in the back of my delivery van. We were parked behind a Kragen Auto Parts. In a gesture toward civility and romance, I brought condoms and a clean blanket. I spent a long time tracing the scars on her knees and elbows, while we detailed our sexual history. My drab list of monogamies held no interest for either us.

When it was her turn, she said, "What do you want to hear about first—rapes or abortions?"

She was my angel! In reality there was nothing that harrowing, but she considered herself the chief of sinners. She had been a skater in her youth, a parking lot rat, an honorary boy, watching her skater friends filming their failed attempts to pull off moves. When she was fifteen she started sleeping with an older boy, and the rest of her comrades looked deeply betrayed. Their goofball demeanors vanished and they started treating her with unbearable deference. She moved on to guitar players and when she was twenty-two she snuck backstage at a Dinosaur Jr. show and gave a blow job to a member of one of the opening bands. She told me about this part of her life with rote precision, as if I were a stranger she would never see again. Once again, I got the sense that she was testing me, waiting for me to look disgusted and go away, but she had grossly overestimated her own depravity. Her exploits would've constituted a single weekend for some of the people who came through the castle. Instead, all I could think about were the later years, after the skaters and musicians, when she was alone in her hometown, heartbroken, paralyzed, her life drifting away, watching TV with her alcoholic father, and it was this pristine vision of spinsterhood that I wanted to save her from. I was twenty-three years old.

I wasn't around the castle much. Javier and Gilbert were excited for me and wished me the best. Nathan didn't seem to notice that I was gone. One afternoon, as I was sitting on the couch, feeling dreamy and spent, Mark walked into the apartment and threw a lemon at my head.

"When do we get to meet your crone?" he asked.

I told him to fuck off and the next day he pawned my dulcimer. I miss those days. Nothing like that happens anymore.

Karen needed money. She called her old music school and they were glad to hear from her. They had contacts in the L.A. area, and promised to keep her in the loop on any other opportunities. Because it was summer, she could tutor kids in the afternoons and still work her night shifts. I picked up extra shifts and registered for classes, once again, at Cal State Los Angeles. I started slowing down whenever I saw a "For Rent" sign in the window of a nice apartment. For a couple weeks we saw less of each other, and the less we saw of each other, the more we wanted to be together.

"I miss you," she said one night over the phone, sounding disappointed in herself.

"Let's get a place."

I was down at the liquor store. Sunset was choked with evening traffic; I could barely hear her, but I knew she was laughing at me. I didn't care that we had only known each other for a couple months. I kept imagining us on a nice couch, listening to records.

"You wouldn't want to live with me," she said.

"Yes, I would."

"I'm a mess," she said. "I'm better off living alone."

"No one's meant to live alone. I won't let you."

Tired of the van, we took over Maria's master bedroom, upstairs. Her husband had carved the four-poster bed himself. A giant crucifix hung over the dresser. We would spend hours

in bed, talking and staring at the bronze Christ. On some eve-
nings, when Karen didn't have to be anywhere, she would sit
down and play the piano. This was the only time in my life that
I listened to classical music. Nocturnes, she said, sounded
best on a Bösendorfer. Maria always requested Chopin, which
Karen played in a trance. Sometimes I'd take Maria out to the
back patio to get some fresh air, and the music sounded even
better from a distance. In those moments there was a shape
to the summer heat; I felt like I was discovering something
that had always been around me, but that I had never noticed
before.

Most of her clients were in Santa Monica. On my days off I
drove Karen to her appointments. Usually I would drop her off
and go to the beach or a record store, my two compass points,
but one afternoon she asked me to come up and meet the family she was working for. The Teagues lived north of Wilshire in
a house with a bright Mediterranean facade. Fountains, pillars,
cypress trees. The Teague boys, six and eight, were handsome
and earnest, just like their mother, Andrea, who wasn't much
older than Karen. They had become friendly, and Karen often
stayed at their house for dinner. As Karen gave the boys their
lessons, Andrea showed me around the house and pointed out
the kitchen window to the pool, a peferct square of turquoise
surrounded by sharp green hedges. It was a picture of the future
I wanted. I would live with Karen and we would have a pool.

"You and Karen can come swimming anytime you want,"
she said.

"Thanks," I said, but I knew I didn't want to swim in *their*
pool.

"She's been through so much," said Mrs. Teague, like she
was talking about a refugee. For a moment I hated this woman,

her dramatic, condescending tone. But then, opening a bottle of wine, she said, "She's told me all about you, Brian."

"Really?"

"She says you're good to her."

This felt like a letdown, but later, as we sat in traffic on the 10, Karen absently took my hand. The sky had turned pink behind the Hollywood Hills.

"You're the only thing I'm good at," I said.

I waited for her to laugh, but instead she curled her fingers into mine.

A few weeks later we drove out to my parents' house in Pomona. My mom had sounded worried when I told her how old Karen was, but not long after we arrived, I became totally redundant to the proceedings. Karen immediately started telling my mom about her mom, dead now for six years. She talked about her mom's fight against cancer in the same tone she had told me about the sexual exploits of her youth. Spilling it all out and waiting for my mom to flinch in disgust. My mom, who had lost her brother and several close friends to cancer, never flinched. They talked and talked, and I just sat there, listening as they eventually moved on from the topic of death to the topic of me. They formed an instant consensus about my shortcomings as a human being. My mom pointed to my baggy shorts and T-shirt.

"He walks around like he's shipwrecked," she said.

"He's a bigger slob than me," Karen said, looking thrilled. It was an ambush.

My dad, who had been outside most of the day working the grill, looked at me with sympathy. But I didn't want it. I had never felt happier. I imagined Karen and my mom running errands together, buying dishes at Target. My mom eventually did this, just a few weeks ago, with another girl, my fiancée.

That night we rented a movie. Karen sat next to my mom on the love seat. My dad sat in his recliner and I had the couch to myself. Halfway through, Karen had fallen asleep with her head on my mom's shoulder. The next day I called my mom and asked if she could loan me some money for us to put a deposit on a place, but she refused.

"She's a sweet person," she said. "But you're too young to be involved with her."

In late August, through the good offices of the mod freak whom Nathan had chatted up a couple months earlier, the Map got a chance to open for Stereolab at the Troubador. I told Karen about it, reluctantly, and she was excited to go. She wanted to meet my friends. When I picked her up, she was wearing a tight black dress. I hardly recognized her. Driving down Santa Monica Boulevard, I started to get knots in my stomach. She had already copped to some youthful starfucking and now, grimly and pathetically, I anticipated her reaction to Nathan. Though not a star, he qualified as some form of cosmic debris. I took a few wrong turns, my goal to make us late for the Map's set.

"You just went in a circle."

"I'm a little lost."

"What's wrong with you tonight?"

"Nothing."

"It might be nice if you told me I looked nice."

I never thought she cared about that kind of thing. I loved that about her.

"You look nice."

"Fuck you," she said quietly, in a resigned voice.

I pulled over and we talked. I told her I was worried she would like my friends more than me and that after tonight everything would become tangled and weird.

"I like that it's just you and me," I said. "I like being alone with you."

She reminded me that her whole life, whether she was skating, in a band, or clearing trees after a storm, she was always part of a crew, always the only girl.

"It's a platonic gangbang," she said. "Then eventually I feel obligated to pick a body out of the pile. And then everyone hates me for it."

"Do you like being alone with me?"

"I don't mind it."

Nathan was outside the club, interrogating one of the club promoters. I got his attention and he pointed to the marquee.

"They didn't put our name up," he said, flicking his cigarette in the gutter like some doomed antihero in a French movie. He started walking back into the club.

"Nathan, this is Karen."

He gave her a brief nod. "Have you seen Mark? We're setting up right now."

I ignored him and we walked inside the empty club. I saw Javier fiddling with his drum kit. I waved to him and he jumped off the stage to say hello.

"Karen, I'm buying you a drink," he said, taking her by the arm. "They gave us tickets for the bar, so it's free."

Gilbert joined us, waving politely to Karen, and we watched people slowly trickle in.

"I'm the oldest person here," said Karen.

"It's an all-ages show," I said.

"Our Aunt Felicia is coming tonight," Javier told Karen.

"She's probably way older than you." He looked around the room, stupefied by history. "The Byrds played here."

Nathan found us and announced that the Map wouldn't go on until the crowd got bigger. "Where the fuck is Mark?"

"Calm down," said Javier.

After a while the club promoter came over and told them they had to start right now. Two other opening acts were waiting to go on. Nathan bravely refused, and the promoter gave the old throat-slash signal to somebody we couldn't see. Suddenly a bunch of tech guys rose up from the shadows like ninjas and began dismantling their gear. Javier ran over and begged them to stop, but it was too late. Nathan started screaming at the promoter and there was some pushing and shoving. Security removed Nathan from the premises. Karen and I helped them get their gear down from the stage. For a moment I paused and looked down at a few bright faces—curious and devoted kids who had come early to watch every band, even the ones they had never heard of.

Nathan sat on the bumper of his station wagon, crying. The girl who had once disappeared into the photo booth was trying to console him.

"I'm sorry, guys," Nathan said.

"Maybe you could help us load the stuff," said Javier.

Nathan looked around. "Where's Mark?"

The night turned out fine. We went to a couple bars. Aunt Felicia bought everybody a round. I cheered Nathan up by reminding him that Harry Nilsson and John Lennon once got thrown out of the Troubador. Javier went crazy when Karen told him the name of her old ska band. He actually owned one of their old seven-inches. Later we got food at Denny's. Karen kept her hands folded in her lap and drank her Coke by leaning her whole body toward the straw. After taking a sip, she shivered a little and rubbed her hands on her knees. She whispered in my ear that she missed nights like this, eating in a diner, with everyone telling stories and reaching for the wrong glass of water. Walking home, Karen put her arms around me. We played *GoldenEye* until five in the morning, at which point Mark came home stoned and shirtless and carrying a guitar that he had stolen from one of the other opening acts. Everyone went to bed. There's plenty of room on a single for two drunk people, and we slept comfortably.

A month later Karen accepted a teaching job at a music school in Bermuda.

They needed a new teacher and could pay a generous salary. Despite its paradisiacal qualities, nobody, it seemed, wanted to move to Bermuda. They said she came highly recommended from her old instructors at the Berklee College of Music. They offered to fly her out to meet the faculty and explore the island. She agreed to go, just as a lark, scamming a free trip to a tropical island. She even asked if she could bring her boyfriend along, but they said that wasn't possible. She had just started to do some recording with the Map. Nathan asked her to play keyboards live, but she refused. The day she left I picked her up at their rehearsal space—an insulated garage somewhere in Chinatown that Mark had found—and everybody wanted to go along. We had to take Nathan's station wagon to LAX. She promised to bring back souvenirs.

I knew she would take the job. In those last few weeks, when she was around the castle playing video games or listening to records, she would sometimes look at all of us with a terrible sense of recognition, like someone lost in the woods who sees a familiar landmark and realizes she's been walking in circles. Still, I started to imagine our life together in Bermuda.

A week later I got a letter, postmarked in New London, Connecticut. She was taking the job. She felt horrible and didn't want to face coming back to L.A. and seeing me. She flew straight home and was now taking care of paperwork before moving to Bermuda for good. For the first couple months she was going to stay with the same family who'd put her up during her visit. She went on and on about the crystal-blue waters surrounding the island, as if this explained everything. At the end she mentioned that we should break up.

If she had just moved back home, or back to New York, or almost anywhere else, I might've accepted it, somewhat graciously. But she didn't. She moved three thousand miles away to a quasi-fantastical island in the middle of the ocean.

In late October she started writing me letters. The envelopes were sky-blue, crisp, and weightless, with a royal postage stamp and a checkered fringe. I still have these letters, not because I've been pining for Karen for ten years, but because they are the last real letters anyone has ever sent me. I like the way they feel in my hands. Even then her letters felt antiquated, as if they had arrived from a lost age of steamships and parasols. She asked about the band, my mom, Maria. She wrote long rhapsodic passages about the color of the water and the barracudas she had seen darting among the reefs. She then offered a few words to the effect that she missed me and loved me, that she was lonely and regretted the move, that she hated the British and wanted to leave but they were paying her and she had signed a contract and everything was so expensive in

Bermuda she still couldn't really get ahead and was there any chance I could visit.

I resumed my stewardship of the phone bill and called her. After a three-hour conversation we were officially back together. I told my roommates and we all went out and got loaded. I called her a couple more times and I sent some letters. She couldn't wait for me to come to Bermuda. There were so many beautiful things she wanted to show me. She was now subletting a studio in Hamilton for $900 a month. I could stay with her as long as I wanted. My phone bill was over $300, almost twice my rent. I wrote Karen asking if she could call me sometimes, but she said she couldn't afford it. Slowly, I noticed the tone changing in her letters. After some remorse it was obvious she was starting to settle there, hating it less and less. She went on and on about the water. Apparently it was very blue. Now when I talked about visiting after Christmas, she said only if I wanted to, and only if I could afford it. I picked up more shifts at work. Three weeks passed without a letter. Finally, she wrote to say that she couldn't live in two places at once. There was no return address on the envelope. I thought this was a little too dramatic, like Maria Recoba declaring her wish to die.

A couple weeks before Christmas, Mark agreed to come with me to Maria's house. She still hadn't sold the piano. Mark explained to her that if she had papers for it, his guy would advance her a fair sum of money and they wouldn't even have to arrange to move the piano into his pawnshop.

"He just needs the papers," Mark said, "and then you get cash right away, while he looks for a buyer." Mark tickled the keys with his fat, troll-like fingers. "This is a beautiful piano and he says he knows people. For most things he'll just sit on it, but this is high-end for him and so he'll actively pursue a sale."

"The papers are in the bench," she said.

As I sat down next to her on the couch, dust billowed up from the cushions.

"Maria," I said, "since I'm kind of arranging everything, I was hoping you could give me a percentage of the sale."

"The money goes to Blessed Sacrament."

"I need money for a plane ticket. I'm going to visit Karen."

She gave us the papers. My cut was exactly the price for a round-trip ticket to Bermuda. I didn't take a penny more. But two weeks later my supervisor called me into her office. Maria, quite innocently, had mentioned our arrangement to one of the caseworkers. I got fired on the spot.

A few days after Christmas Javier and Gilbert and the photo booth girl dropped me off at LAX.

"What if you can't find her?" Javier asked again. He was not a proponent of this trip, which upset me. I was doing something highly poetic, fighting the twin beasts of reality—logic and finance. I wanted to be congratulated.

"It's a small island," I said.

"You've got no money, man."

I was bringing twenty bucks and a disposable camera.

"I'll be fine," I said. "Karen's got money."

"Good luck," said Gilbert, holding the photo booth girl's hand. "If you see her, say hi."

I had never flown before, and Javier's twenty-first birthday in Tijuana was actually the only time in my life I had set foot outside of California. It was a clear morning and when the plane took off it circled over the ocean. For a moment I could see the entire coastline. Then we turned slowly and flew east over the quilted sprawl of Los Angeles. After five minutes I got over the novelty of soaring through the heavens and fell asleep.

During my layover in Boston, I called my mom to tell her I had made it. She too was not a proponent of this trip. She had refused to loan me money for a plane ticket. "What the hell are you doing, Brian?" she asked me for the hundreth time, and I hung up on her.

I boarded a small plane for Bermuda. Sitting to my right, in the window seat, was an older man, a retired banker, who wore a blue blazer with khaki pants and a pair of leather sandals. We talked the entire flight. He went to Bermuda every Christmas to golf and seemed pleased that I was also traveling alone. I told him I was there to do some snorkeling. As the jet came down through the clouds, he let me lean across him and see the island.

"It looks like a hook," I said.

It was probably beautiful, probably the most beautiful thing I've ever seen—the hills green, the water turquoise—but it was too small and precious to be an actual place with roads and people. It seemed roughly the same size as LAX.

"I usually sail from Hingham," he said, "but things didn't work out this year."

We said goodbye on the tarmac, but after I walked out of the terminal and found the bus stop, I heard him calling my name. He was in the backseat of a taxi.

"Are you going to Hamilton?"

"I think so."

"Get in."

It was a cloudy evening. Going over the causeway to the

main island, I saw yachts in the harbor and black seabirds rising from the breakwaters. The taxi swerved down narrow streets that were lined with stone walls. The hillsides were green and dotted with pastel houses, each one with a white limestone roof that rose in steps like a Devo hat.

Streetlamps glowed along Front Street. The taxi pulled up next to a hotel and the driver told us how much. The banker got out his wallet.

"Split it?" he said.

"I thought you were treating."

"I never said that."

"I would've just taken the bus."

"The gentleman's waiting."

"I don't have any Bermudian money."

"They take American money."

"I don't have any of that either."

The banker paid the driver. I got out of the taxi and helped him get his golf clubs out of the trunk. He took a deep breath. "Well, I'm sorry for the misunderstanding," he said. "I just thought we were a team."

We shook hands and said goodbye again. I looked at my map and started walking north up one of the main streets. Everything was smaller in Bermuda. Cars, buildings, people. Karen now owned a metallic blue 1969 Vespa Rally. She'd sent me a picture of it, back when she was still sending pictures, and I had held it aloft to my roommates, proving once and for all that Karen was the queen of the mods, the iciest of crones. I passed a little park and saw two private-school kids in blazers, sharing a cigarette and cursing in their dainty little accents. It started to rain.

The school was in an old colonial building, lime green with

white shutters. The front door was locked. Through the windows I saw a chubby little blond girl being led down the stairs by her mother. They opened the door and I asked her if Karen Kovac was there. She said the only teacher left inside was Mr. Hadley-Rowe. She opened an umbrella, took the little girl by the hand, and they jogged to their little car.

At the top of the stairs I saw a young man with wispy brown hair and fashionable glasses. The nameplate on his door read "Jeremy Hadley-Rowe." He was my age, but wore nice clothes; he was the first hyphenated man I had ever met. I told him that I was a friend of Karen's, and went on to explain in carefully planned detail that because of some miscommunication she missed me at the airport and I just needed her address, that's all.

"You must be Brian."

"I am."

"She said this might happen."

"Where is she?"

"She lives in Somerset now," he said.

Back in November, I had sent my last letter to her Hamilton address, but it got returned. He didn't know her new address in Somerset, but he had been there before.

"Her scooter breaks down a lot," he said. "And her neighborhood's a bit crap. I often give her rides home."

I got out my map and he showed me where she lived and which bus to take. The rain continued as I walked down to Front Street. When my bus came, it was crowded and I had to stand in the middle. The windows fogged up and I couldn't take in the scenery. With all the stops it took forty-five minutes to get into Somerset. I got out and started walking, checking my map over and over. The streets were narrow and lethal. Kids zipped around on Vespas, laughing and screaming. When a car passed, I had to inch along the mossy stone walls to keep from getting hit. It was completely dark when I finally found her street. She lived in a house at the end of a cul-de-sac. I knocked.

A black man with a shaved head answered the door. He was holding an orange cat.

"Does Karen live here?"

"She's in the cottage out back," he said. In the room behind him a boy and girl were sitting on the floor, drawing pictures and watching TV. He stepped onto the front steps and shut the door behind him. He shook my hand.

"You must be Brian."

I nodded.

"I'm Peter, Karen's landlord. She's not here."

"Where is she?"

"Most of her students fuck off back to England for the holidays. She's house-sitting this week for one of the families. This is Sam, her cat."

He held up Sam so I could give him a little scratch under the chin. Peter didn't know where Karen was house-sitting. I asked if there was any chance he could give me a ride back to Hamilton. His wife had the car, he said, but his friend Kano might be able to help. I followed him into the house. As he picked up the phone, his kids looked at me briefly, with total indifference, and returned to their drawing.

"Karen's boy's come around," he told Kano. "He needs a ride." Peter nodded a couple times and hung up. "Go wait at the end of the street. He'll be right there."

"Should I pay him?"

"I don't know. That's up to you."

"Great. Thanks."

The rain stopped. The clouds were breaking up and I could see some stars. When Kano pulled up he told me I couldn't wear shorts on the back of his Vespa.

"You might burn your leg on the motor."

"I don't have any money."

"It's all right. You're Karen's friend."

Karen had added me to her litany of woe, and I wondered if there was anyone on the island who didn't know her sob story.

"I'm not her friend," I said.

I changed into jeans right there on the street. Kano was tall and had to hunch his back to fit on the scooter. He took a shortcut along a stretch of old railroad tracks, his motor cracking the night air as we raced along a corridor of towering stone walls. I would remember my night ride with Kano, whoever he was, as the best part of my trip.

When we got back to Hamilton I asked him to drop me off at the hotel on Front Street. It was the only place I could think to go.

"I thought you didn't have any money," he said.

"I'm not actually staying here."

I felt guilty, so I ended up giving him ten bucks. Kano revved up and disappeared around a corner.

My plan was to wait until morning and then go back to the school. I spent a few hours in the lobby, trying to sleep in a big leather chair. At some point a concierge came by and asked if I was a guest of the hotel.

"Yes," I said.

"What's your name, sir?" he asked.

"Nigel Dickslap."

As a security guard escorted me from the lobby, I saw the banker sitting alone at the hotel bar.

• • •

For the last ten years, when I dream about Bermuda, I dream about this part of the trip, walking aimlessly around Hamilton, trying to avoid the constabulary. I never see Karen. Instead, I just wander around the island, looking for her in the rain, meeting people who say they've seen her. For some reason, in the dreams, I never trust these people.

At one point that night I lay down on a stone bench in a park. I remember waking up cold, but happy to see light coming through the trees. Suddenly I was looking forward to being back in Los Angeles, telling my roommates about my night sleeping outside like a bum in fucking Bermuda! Karen was already becoming an afterthought.

I did end up seeing her, but she had already disappeared.

I splurged on an egg sandwich and waited outside the school until it finally opened at nine o'clock. The secretary told me that Karen wasn't working today. I asked if she knew the family she was house-sitting for.

"The Cavanaughs," she said, her eyes wide with excitement. "She's actually *mansion*-sitting!"

It was a cloudy day. I fell asleep on the bus out to Warwick and went too far. When I woke up the bus was stopped outside an old fort. Tourists walked along the stone ramparts, looking out across the Atlantic. I found an information kiosk that gave a history of the island. In 1503, a Spanish ship had discovered Bermuda, by accident, when it shattered on a reef. I imagined one of these filthy Spaniards, standing alone on the beach, holding a spyglass and dagger.

Back in Warwick, I walked up a street that curled into green hills. I passed a horse stable and, farther along, a golf course. The secretary had given me the Cavanaughs' address, but I didn't need it. Next to the black iron gates their name was embossed in stone. Through the bars I saw a peach-colored mansion. I couldn't knock. Instead, I pushed a red button on the intercom.

"Brian," she said, with that note of resignation in her voice.

I looked around. There was a camera on the fence. I waved. "Can I come in?"

"I don't really have a choice, do I?"

"My plane ticket cost seven hundred dollars."

The gate slowly opened. At the front door Karen took my bag. Walking down the hall a ghost passed over us and we started to kiss, but it didn't last long. She put me in a nice, comfortable guest room with a giant queen bed. From my window I could see white sailboats anchored in the sound. She worked the next few days, while I slept and hung around the house. We had sex once. Her Vespa was broken, but I asked her to take a picture of me sitting on it, so I could show the guys. On my last night there was a full moon and we walked on the beach. I have never been, nor will I ever be, in a more romantic setting. It was complete hell. Back at home she played piano for a few hours, working up a sweat in the humid air, and later we both fell asleep on the couch watching TV. In the morning it was raining and all the buses were running late. After I asked her a few times, she finally loaned me cab fare to the airport. We never talked again and I never paid her back.

Elephant Doors

On tape days, before his escort to the soundstage, Max Lavoy liked to entertain his writing staff with anecdotes from Belgian history. One morning in late spring, with the game scripts spread before him and a can of Diet Rite in his hand, he said:

"Godfrey de Bouillon, the leader of the First Crusade, was, of course, a Walloon."

Adam Cullen, the new production assistant, thought this might be the end, but from there Max did five solid minutes on the royal patronyms of Lower Lorraine. The writers offered up practiced smiles of delight and gratitude, while trying, in subtle ways, to signal Adam, who was circling the table with a box of donuts.

"Last summer in Namur I bought a tapestry with de Bouillon's coat of arms. Argent, a cross potent between four cross-lets . . ."

Adam listened in awe. The content of Max's speech meant nothing to him, absolutely nothing, but he envied the man's chops, his ability to just go on and on, with total conviction that his audience cared.

One of the head writers, Doug Holliday, risked a glance away from Max and caught Adam's eye.

"Sprinkles," he whispered.

Aurora borealis, George Washington, the Magna Carta . . . Doug had spent fifteen years down here in the research library, writing questions for the longest-running quiz show in television history. Like the rest of the staff, his dark eyes and sallow skin testified to a ghoulish mastery of the banal.

Adam reached into the box, looking for a sprinkled donut, but then he heard Max break off.

"What's that, Doug?"

It was quiet. The air became prickly and hot, and though he had only been an official member of the staff for a week, Adam felt a sudden urge to genuflect and apologize for his part in the disturbance. But he wouldn't have to, as Doug took it upon himself to handle the situation.

"Correct me if I'm wrong, Max," he said. "But is Namur part of the Brabant?"

"No, it's not," said Max. "That's a common mistake. Both are part of Wallonia, but Namur is a separate province. Namur—the city itself—is a beautiful place. It's one of those quiet little towns that's been invaded by everybody. The Hapsburgs. Napoleon. And the Germans, of course. Twice!"

There was laughter. As the laughter continued, Max rose from the table. Everybody stood up; they were still laughing. Adam heard himself laugh, though he wasn't quite sure why. Several writers, walking back to their offices, exchanged a furtive salute with Doug.

Melanie Martin, the senior producer, waved to Adam and he ran to her side. A long time ago, with a feathery blond mane, she had played a sickly ingénue on three episodes of *Falcon Crest*. When her character died of pneumonia—or was it murder?—she decided to give up acting and learn the black arts of production. Eventually she landed in game shows and climbed the ranks. She told all this to Adam the day he was officially hired, as a sort of pep talk. Her story was totally canned, but so was everybody's, and Adam didn't mind hearing it. He looked forward to the day when he could regale some-body with his own tale of professional triumph. At fifty, Mela-nie was beautiful and intimidating, and now she was grabbing Adam by the elbow and introducing him, finally, to Max Lavoy.

"This is Adam Cullen, our new production assistant."

"Is it still raining?" Max asked.

"I think so," said Melanie. She cleared her throat. "Adam temped upstairs for a while. He did a great job handling our last ticket promotion."

"I stuffed envelopes for six months," said Adam, with a win-ning note of self-deprecation.

"Somebody give me an umbrella," said Max.

"I don't think you'll need one. Adam will drive you over when you're ready."

"It's nice to meet you, Mr. Lavoy," said Adam, reaching out his hand. He was shocked by the strength of Max's grip. The man had gray hair and a slight stoop in his shoulders, but he was naturally tanned and there was a tautness in his neck that suggested a daily regimen of vigorous activity.

"Tell me your name again," said Max.

"Adam Cullen."

"Cullen. That's Irish."

"It's Gaelic for 'drunk.'"

Nothing. Max just stared at him. Adam instantly regretted the foray into humor. Max finished his soda and handed the empty can to Adam. "Well, I'm ready."

Adam's new badge was blue and gave him access all over

the studio lot. He swiped it and opened the door for Max. On his way out he glanced back at Melanie, who put a finger to her lips like a librarian, gently demanding silence.

After so many years of success, raking in millions for the studio, the show had the authority to budget certain outrageous luxuries, like a golf cart made up to look like a black Mercedes-Benz. Adam now had access to the Benz and he used it to ferry his precious cargo through a light drizzle. Other golf carts, less deluxe, buzzed up and down the narrow lanes between soundstages. He received honks of recognition from studio messengers, production assistants, and other members of the squire class. Then he passed one guy who was on foot. Adam had once temped with this guy at another production company on the lot. Adam couldn't remember his name, but he saw that he still wore a red temp badge. Hence the walking—temps, for insurance reasons, couldn't drive the golf carts. The guy waved, but Adam pretended not to see him.

One side of the soundstage was draped with a massive banner, forty feet high, that featured the looming gaze of Max Lavoy. As he got out of the golf cart, Max paid no attention to the iconography of himself. Adam skipped past Max, swiped his badge, and opened the side door that led to his dressing room.

"Do you need anything else, Mr. Lavoy?"

"No, I can manage. I'm not a fucking child."

The door slammed shut behind him.

For the next two hours, as lights were tested and contestants prepped, Adam drove the Benz back and forth between the research library and the soundstage production booth, delivering game scripts and updated schedules for promo shoots. After his last run before taping started, he bumped into Doug outside the office. Doug, on his smoke breaks, always wore a leather gimp mask. It was black with silver zippers. Doug had made friends with all the prop masters on the lot and he kept his office stocked with weird getups. A few years ago he wore the gimp mask outside on a dare, delighting the Teamsters who were lined up at the lunch trunk, as well as a passing tour group, who snapped pictures of him. Doug enjoyed the attention and he wore the mask a few more times. It got to the point that the tour guides began to look for this lurid creature, pointing him out as a hallowed studio legend, like the ghosts that supposedly haunted Stage 21. Doug was now weary of the attention, but he told Adam that he felt an obligation to maintain the facade of wackiness. During Adam's time as a temp, in which he stuffed over sixty thousand envelopes, most of the staff treated him politely, but nobody asked him anything about himself. Doug was the only person who acknowledged the possibility that Adam had a life beyond stuffing envelopes. He had spotted Adam going off to lunch one day with a copy of *The Man Who Was Thursday* in his hand, and a righteous bond was forged.

"Well?" he said.

"I drove around in a golf cart with Max Lavoy."

"Living the dream, bitch."

"I asked if he needed anything else, and he said, 'I'm not a fucking child.' That was the single greatest moment of my life."

"The man is human," said Doug. "Don't forget that."

"When I was growing up my family watched him every night at dinner." Adam pointed to the distant banner of Max. "We'd sit on the couch and shout the answers."

"I hear that a lot."

"I'm stoked."

"You'll get sick of it," said Doug. "And then you'll hate your-self for getting sick of it. I've got five more years guaranteed on my contract. Five years! Nobody in town has that and I still curse God because I haven't sold my pilot."

"I didn't know you wrote a pilot."

"I contain multitudes."

"What's it about?"

"It's called *Paralegals*. It explores the world of paralegals."

"Fuck you. I love it here."

"Yeah, but you're young and stupid. And ugly."

"If you knew some of the jobs I've had."

"I was a writer's assistant on *Mr. Belvedere*."

"Jesus Christ," said Adam.

There was a grim silence, as if Doug had just confessed his role in some infamous wartime atrocity.

"So how'd you end up writing questions for Max?"

"I don't know," said Doug, releasing smoke from his zip-pered mouth. "I sort of failed my way to the top."

He put out his cigarette on the side of his head and went back inside.

Most of Adam's responsibilities involved prep work, so once taping started he didn't have much to do. For a while he checked his email and fantasy sports leagues; then he took out an index card and put together his open mic set for later that night. Trying to perfect one bit, he crossed out the word *cabrón*, replaced it with *puto*, but after thinking about it for a long time, he crossed that out and put *cabrón* back in. It was torture making these kinds of decisions.

He got a free lunch ticket on tape days—the studio perks

were coming thick and fast—and on his walk back from the cafeteria, he stopped by the soundstage to pocket free cookies and watch Max in action.

Black curtains surrounded the gilded set. The wings were hushed and dark and Adam found a place behind the contestant coordinators, who stood poised with hair gel and bottled water. Max, taking his cue, walked over and chatted with the contestants. The first one, a pediatrician from Omaha, flubbed her defining personal anecdote. Max covered his mic and whispered something that made her laugh. It was a polite laugh, but that didn't matter; looking more relaxed, she did fine on the second take, describing a fairly benign misadventure on her honeymoon in Yellowstone, and there was palpable relief in the studio audience. Adam had to give Max credit. Though pompous and strange, he was good at his job. Because they taped five shows a day he only worked about fifty days a year, pulling in ungodly sums of money, but still, everything depended on him, and if he were ever to quit, it would spell doom for everyone on staff, from the executives down to the production assistants.

"Good, you're here," whispered Melanie, suddenly behind him. "Max is out of Diet Rite."

"No."

"Yes, it's true," she said, in a dry, withering tone that Adam loved. "I need you to stock the fridge in his dressing room before this game ends." She handed him the key. "The holiest of holies. Don't linger."

Adam made a lap of the set, first grabbing a twelve-pack from the pantry, and then moving with stealth toward the dressing room, which was just on the other side of the giant blinking game board.

The dressing room had a nice leather couch, a coffee table piled with magazines, and a small closed-circuit television tuned to the live feed of the game currently in progress. There was a large mirror surrounded with lightbulbs, and on the dressing table below it a framed photo of Max with a German shepherd. In contrast to the natural solemnity of the dog, Max's smile was eager and silly. Black-and-white publicity shots covered the far wall, but in these his smile seemed less genuine: Max getting his star on the Walk of Fame, Max with some underprivileged kids, Max hamming it up with Leonard Nimoy.

Adam stocked the mini-fridge and then, for a long time, he just stood there, lingering. Faintly, he heard the final-round theme song begin, which meant that he had at least thirty seconds to take advantage of the blazing mirror. After a medley of bad impressions—Connery, Bronson, Shatner—he did an abridged version of Dirk Diggler's concluding monologue from *Boogie Nights*, but when he got to the grand finale, he decided it would be tacky, in the these circumstances, to pull out his dick.

But he did it anyway.

The door started to open. Adam zipped up and then turned quickly, shamefully, to find a woman holding a blow-dryer and makeup kit. "Who are you?" she asked.

"I'm Adam. The new P.A."

She started to nod, but hesitated.

"Max was out of Diet Rite."

"Oh!" she said brightly, and this seemed to resolve everything. Adam forced a smile and left the room.

At four o'clock, when the final game wrapped, Adam collected all the game scripts and shredded them, for security purposes. The evening mail drop came and he spent a few minutes sorting Max's fan letters. A lovestruck woman in Kalamazoo had decorated her envelope with hearts and question marks. When the last of the senior producers left, he waited five minutes, to give the impression that he was busy and working late, and then he turned off his computer and exited through a back door.

The rain had stopped. A shuttle made the rounds, taking people to the parking structure at the far end of the lot, but Adam preferred the long walk through the giant soundstages. He liked spying on the sets of future blockbusters. Now and then he saw a movie star, but he always got more excited when he identified a character actor. He was proud of this ability, thinking it showed a deeper commitment to the culture.

Adam's car was parked at the top of the structure, which gave him a panoramic view of the city. On most days downtown was obscured by smog and haze, but now, after the rain, he could see the glass towers rising like columns of fire in the evening light. There was even a rainbow, connecting Baldwin Hills to the south and the 10 freeway to the north; it arched over the studio buildings and Adam felt blessed as he noticed something both beautiful and preposterous, the kind of thing that was only possible in Los Angeles. Beneath the rainbow, in the immediate foreground, there was a white windowless warehouse, three stories high, with two giant words painted on the side: "Scenic Backdrops."

Adam drove to El Goof, a beer dungeon on Lincoln Boulevard. It wasn't crowded yet; a few regulars milled around in the darkness, playing *Ms. Pac-Man* and talking with the owner and MC, Frankie "El Goof" Moreno. He was a fellow SoCal, a fat stoner with a stringy black ponytail and one eye that was significantly more bulgy than the other. Adam waved to him.

"I already put you down," said Frankie, holding up his clipboard. "You're going first."

This was Adam's preferred spot—he liked to go first and get it out of the way. Adam thanked Frankie and left to get dinner. He drove one block to Del Taco and spent an hour in the parking lot, devouring his macho-sized No. 1 combo, listening to the Dodgers game, and going over his three minutes.

A homeless man interrupted him, tapping his window and asking if he wanted to buy a copy of *Street Spirit.*

"No, thanks," said Adam. "I read it online."

Nothing. Adam started rummaging for some quarters, but the man had already moved on to other cars waiting in the drive-through line. After a little while, the nerves hit. Adam got out of his car, walked behind a dumpster, and methodically threw up his dinner. This was all part of his Friday routine.

He looked down Lincoln Boulevard, a treeless span of auto body shops, futon outlets, and discount shoe emporiums. Adam savored these sights, knowing that someday, in a nostalgic mood, he would look back fondly on his tawdry origins.

When he returned to El Goof, the place was full, which wasn't unusual on a Friday. Frankie had recently rebuilt the stage and invested in a new PA system that didn't electrocute the talent. Booking agents had started to show up regularly and several people who performed there had landed some nice paid gigs. Adam bought a bottle of Coors Light and took his usual seat next to Sleeper Cell, a sketch troupe made up of Persian degenerates from the Caliphate of Brentwood. They specialized in airport security gags. One of them was insanely talented and had recently moved up another level at the Ground-lings. Adam expected to see him on TV at some point, getting sodomized with a broomstick by Jack Bauer. No one else in the room would be that lucky. Behind him there was a guy named Ramon, who for the last six months had been working on the same bit about the disappointing lack of starring roles for Mexicans: "*Lawnmower Man*—no Mexicans! *The Mexican*—no Mexicans!" It had potential, but he just couldn't get it right. In front of him, a college girl studied her notes, which she kept in her Trapper Keeper. That was one of her jokes, owning a Trapper Keeper. It was ironic. She was supersmart and hip, and on some nights she was easily the funniest person in the room, but she wasted most of her time talking about all the weirdos who stalked her online. One of the stalkers, Adam assumed, was sitting to her right, a pale and neatly groomed bearded man of indeterminate age wearing a stiff pair of jeans and a yellow Izod shirt. He didn't wear a belt on his jeans and typically, instead of jokes, he divulged repugnant details about his personal life. Hemorrhoids, flatulence, the metallic scent of his urine—these were the wellsprings of his comedy. He had the humid lips of a pedophile, and after three minutes of his squint-eyed horror, everyone in the room wanted to go home and take a shower. But Frankie had a democratic spirit and gave everyone a chance to be heard. Favoring his bad leg—an old spearfishing injury—Frankie mounted the stage and did his normal intro.

"Welcome to comedy night at El *Gooooof*!" Frankie was a laid-back guy but he always let loose on the goof. It actually got Adam pumped up. "If you don't know already, everybody gets three minutes. When you see my flashlight, start wrapping up. Please be attentive and respectful. And remember. You're here to entertain the people in front of you, tonight, in this room. If you have a bigger agenda than this room, then congratulations. The exit is right there. We'll see you on *Carson*."

"Carson's dead!" shouted Chris Hobbs, a handsome twenty-three-year-old from someplace back East. Most of his material dealt with his adventures as an earnest young man trying hard to make it in Hollywood. Apparently, during his two months here, he had met a lot of phonies. Also, the traffic drove him nuts. Every time he opened his mouth Adam wanted to carve his face with a broken beer bottle.

"Or *Leno*," said Frankie. "You know what I mean."

"Leno sucks," said one of the terrorists, getting a round of applause.

"He's not so bad," said Frankie. "Dude has to reach a broad audience."

Frankie was basically just a local. He had never done stand-up, which made his solicitude toward the worst people on earth, comedians, a total mystery. After Adam's first set at El Goof, he had been very encouraging, though as time wore on Adam didn't understand why he didn't do more to help, like giving him longer sets or introducing him to booking agents. But Adam knew he was being ungrateful. Every Friday, Frankie sat in the back of his crappy bar, laughing generously and running outrageous tabs. Adam thought of Father Damien among the lepers.

"Okay. Let's have some fun," said Frankie, looking at the clipboard. "Our first comedian tonight is Adam Cullen."

Mandated applause. Adam rising from his squeaky folding chair, floating down a tunnel of light. Frankie with a pat on the shoulder. Up the steps, beer in hand, and then the turn, facing the audience, a dark treacherous bog. On a dead run: "I finally found the self-help book that's going to unlock my potential. It's called *Mein Kampf*." Nothing, absolutely nothing. Only Frankie with a squeal of delight. "I've got the audiobook on my iPod and it really gets me going when I'm doing hills on the elliptical." Coughs, bottles sliding back and forth on tables. Pausing. A fatal mistake opening with Hitler. Still paused. "Um." Peeking at the index card. "Fine. Let's have some fun. We'll play the dozens. Here we go. Yo mama so fat . . . she died of complications from diabetes." Thirty faces cringing. "More? Sure. Yo mama so stupid . . . she was declared legally retarded and made a ward of the state. Her kids are now in foster care. It's a vicious cycle, people." Too grim, too grim. "On weekends I play soccer in the park with some of my friends from the Honduran immigrant community. They love me and they've given me a nickname—*cabrón*, which I believe is Spanish for 'champion.'" A few ripples out there. Strike with pathos. "The worst job I ever had was clerk at a party supply store. It was like being alone on my birthday five days a week." That's right. Feel the joy. "Um." *Ms. Pac-Man* pinging in the back. To the index card. Looking for something to please the rabble. "Do you know what I like most about pornography? The raw and explicit content." Nothing. "Plus the whimsical sense of humor that presides over the industry. You know, the way porn titles make puns on Hollywood movies. I saw a great one the other day for *The Matrix*. It was called *Teenage Ass Sluts Volume Ten*." Wretched and obvious, longest setup in history. Keep going. "Maybe I don't quite know what a pun is, but that's because I was educated on the streets." Sip of domestic beer. "Of New Haven, Connecticut. I graduated from Yale with a degree in economics." A car alarm outside. "Um." Um. Fuck. Um is doom. "Um." Playing with the mic cord. Red-faced.

Sinking into the bog. "Thank you." Giving up, before Frankie even flashed his light.

Adam took his place in the audience and clapped mechanically for Hobbs, who bounced up onstage.

"What's up!" he shouted, and from there he gave a blow-by-blow account of his recent audition for a webisode of *Smallville*. Adam tried to be attentive and respectful, but he had collapsed in on himself and after a while he didn't hear a word Hobbs said. He got up quietly and went to the bar, where Frankie bought him a beer.

"*Mein Kampf,*" whispered Frankie, smiling and giving Adam a big thumbs-up.

"Thanks, man."

Adam finished his drink and left in a sulky mood. He felt guilty not staying for the people who had endured his set, but not that guilty, because solidarity was not a watchword among these people.

Driving home, he couldn't see the city. He could only see himself, from the perspective of the audience, witnessing his every weak-minded pause, his every false gesture. He had been putting himself through this for almost two years and he had nothing to show for it. No agent, no booked gigs, nothing. He thought of all the people who had been regulars at El Goof when he first started going, how he would suddenly notice, after a few weeks, that they were no longer there. At some point they had vanished, melting back into the general population. He felt sorry for these people, especially the ones who actually had talent, but after a bad night onstage he often wondered if there wasn't something deeply satisfying in their decision. At times he craved the sweet tantalizing oblivion of giving up. His favorite word in the English language was "stick-to-it-iveness," but the longer he hung around, the more he felt the enormity of his delusion. A voice in his head kept taunting him with the old gambling adage—*if you can't spot the sucker at the table, it's you*—which seemed like an intensely American piece of wisdom. He always figured that being aware of his own suckerhood would somehow redeem him from it, but now he wasn't so sure. He was waiting for something to click. In books and interviews all of his comic heroes had described a moment onstage when, after stumbling for many years, they suddenly, and oftentimes inadvertently, became themselves. Now and then he touched the contours of his own personality, the one that seemed to entertain his family and friends; but most of the time he felt totally disembodied. The words coming out of his mouth seemed like they could've been coming out of anyone's mouth. He was desperate to become who he was, to not care what others were thinking, to dissolve the world around him. He decided that this elusive state of being demanded either total humility or total narcissism. Right now Adam existed in a no-man's-land between the two.

He spent the weekend trying to forget the disappointment of Friday night. He Swiffered his studio apartment in Mar Vista, and then sat down on his futon with a fresh notepad and tried to work on some new bits. He hated topical humor, and the heady, off-kilter stuff wasn't working either, so he tried to think of things from his own life that might be used for material. After a while he remembered an incident from his days as a gas station attendant. One afternoon, as he stood by the pumps, with a squeegee in his hand, a man in a BMW handed him twenty bucks for gas and said, "Why don't they just train a monkey to do your job?" Adam didn't have a comeback then, and he didn't have one now. It was just another random moment of humiliation. He put his notepad down, opened a beer, and proceeded to watch six hours of *The X-Files* on DVD. Saturday seemed to drag along, and then, on Sunday evening, something strange happened. Around six o'clock, as the light was fading, he noticed a distinct lack of dread for the coming week. Instead of wallowing in regret for having accomplished nothing in his life—his favorite Sunday pastime—he was actually looking forward to getting up in the morning and going to the studio. For the first time, his *job* felt like the escape.

It was a quiet week, with no tapings scheduled. Adam ran his normal errands, zipping around the lot in his Benz. One section of the studio featured a fabricated Main Street, with shops and a town square. The old-timey buildings, once fa-cades, were now used as administrative offices. Adam liked to eat lunch in a little courtyard just off Main Street. Most of the casting offices/eugenics labs were here, providing un-canny thrills. On Tuesday, Adam watched an anxious group of teenage girls, all blond, standing in line outside one office, clutching their headshots. On the landing above, a dozen thirtysomething brunettes were striding into another office.

"Adam," said a voice.

He looked up and saw the guy he used to temp with. "Hey," he said, hoping that would be enough.

The guy was nicely dressed in crisp slacks and a collared shirt. Adam didn't have to dress like that anymore, now that he was full-time. He wore jeans and a T-shirt to work. The guy said he was now temping in corporate, in the clearance depart-ment, whatever that was.

"If you guys have another ticket promotion," he said, "maybe you could get me in there."

"Sure," said Adam. "Maybe."

"Do you have my email?"

"I think so."

"Great. Let me know."

"Sure. I mean, there's probably nothing I can do," said Adam. "But still. Yeah."

After lunch, Melanie called Adam into her office and handed him a thick white manila envelope.

"This needs to go to Max's house," she said.

"Do you want me to call the studio messenger?"

"No, Max doesn't trust them. You need to drive it to his house." She wrote down the address. "There's no gate. Just ring the doorbell."

"What is this?"

"Paperwork for one of his charities."

Adam read the seal on the envelope. "What's the St. Maurice Foundation?"

"It provides assistance to Walloon-Americans affected by Katrina."

Adam laughed, but Melanie looked serious. On a bookshelf behind her there was an autographed picture of Robert Foxworth.

"He stuck me on the board of directors so I have deal with it," she said. "Have Max sign these and bring them back. Tell him if he has any questions he can call me. And make sure you take down your mileage. We give you thirty cents per mile."

"Cha-ching."

"Yes, cha-ching. Hopefully, you'll get there before Max's afternoon jog. Go."

Driving north into the Hollywood hills, Adam saw Max twice, in billboard form. He crossed Sunset and gunned his gray Saturn along the shady curves of Laurel Canyon. He turned left at some point and drove for a few miles along a barren ridge. He had envisioned Max living in a baronial manor, his sprawling grounds lush with topiary and crisscrossed by wayward stags, but the ridge just became more and more narrow and the houses lining the road were increasingly modern-looking. Hanging above the dusty canyon, they didn't occupy any land, really, just empty space. Adam reached the address. The view of the house from the road consisted almost entirely of the garage. It was a fancy, modern-looking garage, charcoal-gray with a door that was white and opaque, like a pearl. Next to the garage there was a smaller pearl-white door, and Adam took this to be the front entrance. He walked down concrete steps, past a concrete planter overflowing with star jasmine, and pushed a silver button. A few seconds later Max opened the door wearing dark blue running shorts and a teal tank top. He was barefoot.

"Are you a messenger?"

"No."

"I don't deal with studio messengers."

"I'm not a messenger."

"Liars and cowards. All of them."

"I'm Adam, the new P.A. Melanie sent me."

"Good." He put out his hand. "Nice to meet you."

Once again, Adam was impressed by his grip. He handed Max the envelope.

"Wait here," said Max, and he closed the door. Then it quickly reopened. "Actually, come in. I need your help."

Adam took a step forward, but Max put a hand on his chest and pushed him back with force.

"Take off your shoes."

Adam put his Chuck Taylors on a metal rack just inside the door and followed Max into the house. Steps of polished wood led down to a bright and sparsely decorated living room. A sleek sectional couch, gray with burgundy throw pillows, was placed in the middle of the room, facing a glass coffee table and a floor-to-ceiling glass wall that offered stunning views of the canyon. Behind the couch there were two metal bookshelves packed with thick hardcovers from the sixties and seventies, their plastic spines gleaming in the sunlight. The walls were white and empty, except for Godfrey de Bouillon's coat of arms. Adam was struck by the contrast between the medieval tapestry and the house's modern design. It seemed just right. He tried out a couple vague architectural terms in his head: Modular? Orthogonal?

"This is great," said Adam.

Max turned around, looking slightly confused, as if he weren't sure who was talking. "What?"

"Your house is beautiful."

Max nodded and made a quick slicing motion with his hand. "Clean lines. That's what I wanted. *Clean lines*. Have you heard of the painter Paul Delvaux?"

"No."

"Nobody has. Which pains me. His grandnephew designed this house. Based on my own imaginings."

Max turned the corner into the kitchen and sat down at a small alcove desk, which had another framed photo of Max and the German shepherd. Max opened the envelope, spread out the papers, and started signing them. For a while he seemed to forget about Adam, who leaned casually against the granite countertops; but then, catching himself, he stood up straight, trying to look attentive and respectful. He could see a ghost of himself faintly shadowed in the stainless steel refrigerator. At his feet were five or six grocery bags full of empty soda cans, all of them Diet Rite. Behind Max the glass slider was open, letting in a breeze that brought tidings of a dead skunk somewhere in the canyon. Outside there was a large cast-iron table on the balcony, but next to it only one chair. Adam kept waiting for someone to join them from another room, a wife, a child, a maid, but the house was quiet. Max was alone here, prospering in the eerie stillness of a Tuesday afternoon.

Adam looked at his watch and wondered how long he would have to wait. He couldn't decide if this felt like a privilege or a chore. It was fun standing in the kitchen of a famous man, but he worried that, even just standing there, he was doing something wrong. It was probably rude, he thought, not asking Max more questions about himself. He couldn't think of anything to ask, so he continued to stand there, stiff and mute. Max quietly examined every page, reading the fine print, making checkmarks; but then, suddenly, he raised his head and grabbed a spiral notebook that was sitting on the desk next to his charity documents.

"You mean this?" said Max.

"What?" said Adam. "I didn't say anything—"

"Just a bit of *divertissement*," said Max, shrugging. He stood up. "Do you know who Ravaillac was?"

"No."

"He was an assassin. He killed Henry IV of Navarre, which helped precipitate the Thirty Years' War. Of course, this had a lasting effect on the Low Countries, both good and bad." Max opened the refrigerator and grabbed a Diet Rite. "Do you want one?"

"Sure."

Max closed the refrigerator, opened his soda, and leaned against the counter. Adam wasn't sure if Max had heard him or if he was supposed to just grab his own soda. He decided to stay put.

"I'm addicted to the stuff," Max said. "I know it's a big joke at the office. They think I don't know, but I know." Max took a long gulp of his soda and wiped his mouth. "Now, we're talking about a fascinating moment in history. Dueling monarchies, religious turmoil, it was all happening. And into the middle of it stepped a frothing lunatic named Ravaillac."

He paused for another gulp, and then said, "Am I writing a book? Yes, of course, but sometimes I think, why bother? Who would read it? A few specialists maybe, but so what?"

Max crushed the empty can, tossed it into one of the grocery bags, and for the next hour he set the scene in seventeenth century Europe, describing the lineage of all the major players and their subsequent territorial disputes. Adam dimly followed the action. The Hapsburgs were involved and, apparently, so was the Margrave of Brandenburg. Henry IV, the King of France, sent a cipher to somebody—Gustavus Adolphus?—saying he was planning war against the Hapsburgs. But Hapsburg agents intercepted the cipher, decoded it, and made plans to assassinate him. The phone rang, but Max, on a roll, didn't seem to hear it. As he flipped through his notebook to double-check something, Adam marveled at his small and intricate handwriting. The margins were filled with notes and each page was richly adorned with umlauts and cedillas.

"On the afternoon of May 14, 1610, Henry was riding along the Rue Saint-Honoré in his coach—while the grand machinery of an enemy kingdom was plotting his demise, and while his own army was planning a massive strike—when, out of nowhere, Ravaillac, a complete nonentity, who had absolutely nothing to do with the Hapsburg plot, jumped into the coach and stabbed the king to death with his rapier!"

Max burst out laughing. Adam started to laugh too, but the phone rang again and Max's eyes narrowed in annoyance. He put down his notebook and handed Adam the papers he had signed. "The recycling," he said, snapping his fingers at the bags. "Help me bring them out to the bins. Otherwise it's ant city in here."

Adam picked up half the bags and Max sat down at the desk.

"Through there," he said, pointing. "Open the garage and drag the bins to the end of the driveway." He picked up the phone. "What the fuck do you want, Joanne? It's two in the afternoon."

The smell of skunk was especially strong in the garage, which was vacant except for the trash and recycling bins. Adam, in his argyle socks, couldn't see a single drop of oil on the cement slab. He dumped the bags and went back to the kitchen for the rest. Max was pacing back and forth, holding the portable phone to his ear.

". . . I thought you were going to honor our agreement. Yes, Jo Jo, we did have an agreement . . ."

Adam quietly left the kitchen. After dumping the last bag, he opened the garage door and dragged both bins to the end of the short driveway. When he turned around, he saw Max standing at the back of the garage. He was still on the phone. Max waved cheerfully to Adam and pushed the button, closing the door.

Adam waited for a moment and then walked back to his

car. He wanted to ring the doorbell to ask for his shoes back, but he didn't want to make things awkward for Max.

Adam parked and made his way through the soundstages to the office. He figured if he was walking around in socks, everyone on the lot would be staring and wondering what had happened to him, but no one seemed to notice. Melanie was on the phone when he brought her the envelope. She immediately hung up. "Is everything all right?"

"Sorry it took so long. Max invited me in and we talked for a long time."

"That's a first! He must like you."

"I didn't do anything," said Adam. "I just sort of stood there."

"Well, yeah. But that's great." She arched her eyebrows. "Maybe if we're lucky you'll stick around."

Adam felt himself blush. He adored Melanie. When he got the job, Adam had confessed his creative ambitions, something he had always kept hidden from his other employers like a preexisting medical condition. As a former actress, she understood the necessity of his double life, but now he couldn't quite read her tone. Did she actually think it was only a matter of time before he departed for a brighter world, or was she gently preparing him for the daily grind of this one?

"This is the best job I've ever had," said Adam.

"Five years guaranteed," said Melanie. "Nobody in television has that."

Later, Adam made a run in the Benz, delivering a box of tapes to the postproduction facility, where the editors worked in perpetual shadow. He walked down a darkened hallway, passing every few feet through a penumbra of soft blue light. It felt like an aquarium and the editors, with their sluggish movements and wide, unblinking eyes, were like those strange fish that live at the bottom of the ocean. Adam entered one of the editing bays and quietly dropped off the tapes. The editor, a squat man in his fifties with headphones on, who had spent nearly two decades appending applause to the image of Max Lavoy, looked at Adam, slowly, without expression, and returned to his work.

On the drive back, he ran into Doug, who was wandering around in his gimp mask.

"What are you doing?" Adam asked.

"Getting some exercise."

"Do you want a ride?"

Doug got in and Adam told him about his trip to Max's house.

"He talked about the Thirty Years' War, or the buildup to it, anyway."

"Did he do his whole thing on Ravaillac and Oswald?"

"Oswald? Wow. He didn't get to that. The phone rang."

"That's lucky."

"No, I was sort of into it. I mean, not really, not at all, but still. His voice. It's so smooth. He's got that flow."

"When he talks about what he likes talking about, he sounds like he knows what he's talking about. But I guess that's true of everybody."

"Who's Joanne?"

Doug turned quickly. "His ex-wife. Holy shit—did he actually talk about her?"

"No. She called while I was there. Max got pretty upset on the phone."

"They divorced a while ago, but I don't know much about it. Nobody does. Max is pretty guarded about his private life. Which I admire."

"Me too."

"But if you happen to find out something, I'd love to hear about it."

"Of course."

They turned a corner and found themselves in a traffic jam involving a catering truck and a Teamster flatbed loaded with two giant spools of black cable, and another truck pulling a star trailer. Everyone started honking and yelling.

"You'll lose this battle," said Doug. "Pull in through the elephant doors."

Adam didn't know what he meant at first, but then, turning around, he saw the giant open doors of an empty soundstage and had a sudden flash of intuition. He imagined some harrowing production from the Golden Age, a frazzled director with slick hair and a megaphone, trying to coax a pack of elephants onto his set.

"That's lingo from the old days, right?" Adam said, spinning the steering wheel. "The doors have to be big enough to fit elephants."

"The doors have to be big enough," said Doug, "to fit the egos of the men who walk through them."

"Who said that?"

"I said that."

"No," said Adam. "That sounds like something somebody said."

"Maybe it is. I don't know. I don't have a single original thought in my head."

They took a spin around the dark soundstage. Adam floored

the Benz and did a long skid out on the slick concrete slab, scaring off some pigeons nesting in the catwalks. A security guard walked through the doors, her figure cast in silhouette against the blazing square of light; but once she saw Doug—everyone on the lot recognized Doug when he had his mask on—she gave them the high sign to continue. They got in a few more nice skids and then drove around in circles for a while.

"There's a lot of rich history around here," said Doug, lighting a cigarette. "Did you know this is the soundstage where they filmed *Anaconda II: The Hunt for the Blood Orchid*?"

The next day, at three o'clock, Adam's phone rang. He was busy making copies for one of the publicists; as the papers collated, he did punch-ups for his set later that night. On the third Wednesday of every month, one of the big comedy clubs on Sunset held a lottery for amateurs. If your name was picked out of a hat, you got two minutes before the early show, and if the promoters liked it, you got called back to open the late show. You paid ten bucks for a ticket in the lottery, and if you didn't get picked, the ticket got you into the late show, a consolation prize that nobody wanted. So far Adam's name had never been pulled out of the hat. Every time he lost out he felt foolish and vowed never to go back. But he always went back.

Adam picked up the phone on the last ring.

"It's me," said a familiar voice.

"Mr. Lavoy?"

"Is this you?"

It sounded like a trick question. Adam said, "Yes."

"The one from the other day."

"It's me. Adam."

"What you have to understand is that all our modern assassins descend from Ravaillac. One of the first men to understand this was Philippe Sonck. Have you read Sonck?"

"No."

"That doesn't surprise me. Nobody reads Sonck, and yet he's probably the greatest spy novelist that Belgium ever produced. His oeuvre charts the history of continental espionage, from Cardinal Richelieu to Reinhard Gehlen. *The Lost Tide* is probably his best book. It's all about the final months leading up to the death of Henry IV. There are some historical inaccuracies, and too often he indulges in the kind of baroque flourishes that are *so typical* of the Flemish"—Max laughed softly at his joke—"but it's still a beautiful work of fiction and I'm proud to say that in many subtle ways it anticipates my own imaginings on the subject. Now, listen. You'll like this. In 1928, he sent a letter to his good friend John Buchan. Or was it 1929 . . . ?"

There was a long pause. Adam could hear Max flipping pages. "Yes, I was right: 1928. He told Buchan . . . do you know Buchan?"

Adam felt like he had been given a chance to win some points. He was about to say that, yes, he had read *The Thirty-Nine Steps*, though in truth he had only seen the movie. In any case, he was definitely aware of the work of John Buchan. But before he could say anything Max continued: "This is one of my favorite quotes. Sonck said, 'For the novelist, mood is the only historical truth. Hence the persistence of fog in all our books.'" Max took a deep breath. "Some men just understand things. Do you know what I mean?"

"I'd like to read something by Sonck."

"All his books are out of print," said Max. "Every single one of them."

There was another long pause. Finally, Adam said, "Is there anything I can help you with?"

"Hold on," said Max. "Someone's on the other line. I'll get rid of them."

Adam heard a sharp, piercing tone, and then Max's voice. "Goddammit, Joanne. Not now."

"Mr. Lavoy. I'm not sure you switched over. I think you pushed the wrong button."

"There must be something wrong with the phone. Don't go anywhere."

The line went silent. Ten minutes passed, then twenty, but Adam kept the phone close to his ear. A full hour passed; it was four o'clock and the woman from publicity came into the office to get her copies. Adam apologized for not getting them done.

"I'm on hold with Max," he told her, but she didn't seem to believe him. Later, the line from Melanie's office blinked on and he was afraid to pick it up. After a while she came into the copy room.

"There you are," she said. "Can you run this tape over to post?"

"I'm on hold with Max."

"Is everything okay?"

"I think so. But I have a question for you."

"Sure."

"Who's your favorite Belgian spy novelist? Be honest."

"Oh, God. I'm sorry." She handed him the tape. "Just drop it off whenever he's done."

At five o'clock, Adam decided that Max had forgotten about

him. He hung up, collected his things, and then delivered the tape. On his way to the parking garage he was thrilled to see one of the actors from *Office Space*, the old guy who gets hit by a drunk driver and becomes a millionaire paraplegic.

Adam fought his way up Fairfax and parked on Sunset. A few dozen paranoid comics were already lined up outside the club, trying to improve their chances. Most people, including Adam, suspected that the lottery was rigged by Les Thorpe, a famously mediocre local comic who had taken on a management role with the club, booking shows, handling the amateur hour, and performing other meager tasks that allowed him to stay around the action, if not in it. Adam regarded Thorpe with a certain pity. Despite his pleasant demeanor, Thorpe was suffering in a hell of his own making; he had cashed in his delusions and bought a sad little fiefdom. As Adam got in line, he saw Thorpe emerge from the parking lot, and he wondered if the guy had any idea how little he was respected by the people who befriended him. Adam was determined not to be one of these people; despite all evidence to the contrary, some part of himself—the most vital and destructive part of himself—believed that eventually his talent would be recognized as something pure and triumphant and somehow he would be granted dispensation from the degrading realities that made everyone around him seem so shameless and corrupt. Of course, he had a sinking feeling that everyone around him believed the exact same thing. No rugged, right-thinking American individual would ever admit to kissing ass. That's something the other guy did. It was "networking," nothing more, nothing less. Farther down the line he saw Trapper Keeper from

El Goof and they pretended not to see each other. This was typical. All the sidewalk amateurs tried to maintain an air of aloof self-confidence, but beneath this Adam felt mortal fear, as if they were all racing each other for the last plane out of Saigon. Adam watched Thorpe nice-guy his way down the line, smiling, asking how everyone was doing, laughing with a few regulars who were as mediocre as Thorpe and who therefore seemed to win the lottery with stunning frequency, and then he started collecting his graft and taking down people's names. Someone slapped Adam on the shoulder.

"Hey, man, it's me, Chris!" said Chris Hobbs. "It's you, right?"

"Right."

"This is way better than El Goof! I just found out about it."

Hobbs was too loud, too obvious; everyone turned to look at him and Adam felt suddenly exposed. He had the feeling that all the drivers on Sunset Boulevard were slowing down to laugh at him and all the horrible decisions he had made in his life. He could be out with his old friends, drinking beer in righteous anonymity, but instead he was huddled on the sidewalk with a bunch of miserable strangers. He tried to remember the last time he got a beer with a friend, but he couldn't. "Don't get your hopes up," he said.

"Is that the guy we talk to if we want on the list?" asked Hobbs, who was wearing Elvis sunglasses and a stylish denim shirt embroidered with some kind of Aztec symbol.

"It's supposed to be a lottery," said Adam. "But if you're willing to suck that guy's cock, it'll improve your odds."

There was stifled laughter from a few nearby comics. One of them, through clenched teeth, said, "Dude, be quiet."

"Have you ever gotten picked?" Hobbs asked.

"No," said Adam. "I have too much dignity."

They watched Thorpe stop to chat with Trapper Keeper, who forced herself to laugh at the first thing he said. "We're fucked," said Adam.

Thorpe finally got to Adam and said, "Good to see you, man. How's everything going? You okay?"

"Adam Cullen," he said, with a cold, vacant stare, and for a moment he felt proud of his ability to sabotage himself. But he instantly regretted it and tried to think of something nice to say to Thorpe. He couldn't think of anything in time. Thorpe nodded and wrote down his name. Hobbs leaned forward and in one breath he introduced himself, complimented Thorpe on his shoes, and explained that he had just moved out here.

"Let's do this!" said Hobbs brightly, as Thorpe took his money, and everyone in line, everyone driving down Sunset, everyone in Los Angeles, winced. Thorpe finished taking names and went back inside the club. A few minutes later, he appeared at the front door, called out six names, the usual suspects plus Trapper Keeper, who gave Adam a guilty shrug as she walked inside. Thorpe wished everyone good luck for next time. Those who were kissing ass ten minutes ago were now cursing his name. Adam walked toward his car, but Hobbs caught up with him and asked if he wanted to get some dinner.

"I'd like to pick your brain," he said.

"Why?"

"It seems like you've been around," he said. "You know what you're doing."

"Are you nuts?"

"Please," said Hobbs, and his voice faltered a little. "It's hard meeting people out here." It was almost dark now and he took off his sunglasses. "I'll buy you dinner."

They walked down to a Mexican restaurant. Adam ordered a margarita and a plate of carne asada. Hobbs said he wasn't that hungry, but every time the waiter came around, he asked for more chips and salsa. Hobbs peppered Adam with questions about agents and managers. Instead of admitting his own ignorance and frustration in these matters, Adam gave a speech on the nobility of craft. "If you do things right and put in the work, everything else will take care of itself," he said, with surprising conviction. He felt like he was channeling some future version of himself, the total pro who had attained mastery in all areas of life. Then it occurred to him, with creeping horror, that by summoning this wise man too soon, under false pretenses, he was precluding his existence. He was fucking with the space-time continuum. He imagined the two versions of himself—the young fraud and the old pro—standing on either side of a dark chasm. If there was some blessed third version of himself, the middle man who could bridge the gap, Adam saw no trace of him in the darkness. Rarely had he felt so defeated, and yet here was Hobbs, hanging on his every word. Adam thought he lived at the bottom. But he was wrong. There was no bottom. Adam ordered more margaritas and talked about the first time he heard one of his dad's old George Carlin records. Hobbs admitted that he had never heard any of these, but Adam forgave him, saying that it was dangerous to become overly familiar with the canon. "That kind of knowledge can be a burden," he said. "It can paralyze you."

When the bill came, Hobbs peered despairingly into his wallet. "I only have twenty bucks. I didn't think you'd drink so much."

"Don't worry about it."

"I'm signed up at three different temp agencies," he said. "I can't get anything right now."

Adam, in an expansive mood, paid for everything, explaining to Hobbs that he was actually making good money for the first time in his life. "Sixteen dollars an hour, plus benefits," he said. "There's a three-month probation period, but eventually I'll have benefits."

"I don't have health insurance," said Hobbs.

"What doesn't kill us makes us hopelessly in debt for the rest of our lives."

Nothing. Hobbs just nodded morosely. As they walked back down Sunset, Hobbs asked, "So did I blow it with Thorpe?"

"Don't worry about it," said Adam. "I know things don't look good right now, but in the long run you're way better off than that guy."

"But it wouldn't hurt to get him on my side."

Adam saw a liquor store and popped in. He came back out with a carton of eggs. "Come on," he said. "We're going to do Thorpe a favor."

"What?"

"We'll egg the shit out of his car," explained Adam. "It'll help him reevaluate his life."

Hobbs politely refused. He thanked Adam for dinner and promised to pay him back the next time he saw him at El Goof. They shook hands and said goodbye. Adam watched Hobbs walk quickly down Sunset; he started to jog and then, at the crosswalk, he sprinted away.

By the time Adam got to the parking lot, he had lost his nerve a little. This mission seemed pointless without Hobbs. He suddenly missed the devoted gaze of his pupil. He found

Thorpe's car and saw that someone had beaten him to it. The word "DOUCHEBAG" was scrawled in black Sharpie across the driver's-side door of his Corolla. Adam felt bad for Thorpe, who was somewhere in the club, feeding off scraps. He decided not to throw the eggs; instead, he lined them up, one by one, along the windshield wipers. He figured this would be more effective than egg splatter. Who would take the time to do this? Who would show this kind of menacing restraint? It was surreal and unnerving, the work of a madman. After seeing this, Thorpe would have no choice but to change his life.

With no taping scheduled, the producers took Friday off, so Adam spent most of the day cruising around the lot. Everywhere he looked a stoic Teamster was gathering up electric cable. In one of the soundstages, he witnessed a man spray-painting the udder of a cow, to make it a brighter and more classical shade of pink. Like everyone else who had made it onto the lot, the cow seemed willing to put up with anything.

He found Doug outside, smoking in his gimp mask, and they spent a couple hours throwing a Frisbee around. For a while Adam had fun—he couldn't believe he was getting paid to fuck around on a movie lot—but then he remembered that it was open mic night at El Goof. He didn't want to go. He felt like a kid, on Sundays, waking up to the dread of evening mass.

"How much do you make a year?" Adam asked.

"Don't talk about money," said Doug. "It's vulgar."

"Are you in the Writers Guild?"

"That's where I get all my pussy."

"I want in the Writers Guild."

"Then write something."

"How often do jobs open up here?"

"Not very often," said Doug. He put out his cigarette and looked Adam in the eye. "But if something does, I'll put in a word for you. I know you'd be good at it."

"Thanks, man."

Adam spent the rest of the afternoon putting together his set. At some point earlier in the week it came to him that his studio apartment in Mar Vista had roughly the same dimensions and floor plan as the Unabomber shack. He wrote that down, trying to get something going, and by the time he left the studio he had convinced himself that it was a good bit. He was suddenly excited to get onstage.

When he got to El Goof, Frankie was watching the Dodgers game on mute. There was still some natural light coming through the porthole in the front door and most of the regulars were working on their second or third beer. Adam looked around but couldn't see Chris Hobbs. Last week he had hated him, but now he was actually sort of worried about him. Members of Sleeper Cell were crowded around *Ms. Pac-Man*, cheering each other on. Frankie limped over to Adam, handed him a Coors Light, and picked up his clipboard.

"I'm letting Ramon go first," he said, sounding apologetic.

Ramon, sitting a few stools away, said, "Is that cool?"

"That's fine. I'll go second."

"I have you further down."

Adam looked up from his beer. "How far down?"

"Last."

"Why?"

"Because you keep running out when you're done," said Frankie.

"So?"

"It's not fair to everybody," said Ramon. "We sit through you."

"You do the same shit every week," said Adam. "I don't need to hear it."

"I'm doing new stuff tonight."

"You mean old stuff you haven't done in a while."

Ramon grabbed his beer and walked to the end of the bar. Frankie turned up the sound on the game and then got down in a little crouch so he could address Adam in private.

"You all right?" he asked.

"Sorry. I'll go last. I'll be attentive and respectful toward my peers."

"I know last week was a bummer, but you're really close on a lot of that stuff."

"Close?" Adam snorted.

"An act is like a string of pearls."

"Jesus Christ, Frankie."

"You've got some pearls, but the act is like—"

"The string that holds them together. I *know*."

"Yeah, you've gotta string it the right way." Frankie smiled and rebanded his ponytail. "That's the hard part. Stringing it together. That's what takes time."

"What the fuck are you talking about?"

"It's a string a pearls, man!"

"I get it, but you don't have a fucking clue what you're talking about."

From the end of the bar, Ramon said, "Don't talk to Frankie like that."

"Dude's just blowing off steam," said Frankie, shrugging.

Adam put money on the bar for his beer and stood up.

"That one's on me," said Frankie, pushing back the wadded singles, but Adam wouldn't take them.

"Give my three minutes to Ramon," said Adam, in a loud voice, so everyone could hear him. "Or give it to that sad little fuck."

He pointed to the pedophile, who was sitting alone at a table next to the front door, slowly peeling the label from his bottle of beer. As Adam approached him, he kept his head down and his eyes on the bottle.

"Why don't you just get it over with?" said Adam, standing over him. "Why don't you go home, right now, and kill yourself?"

The pedophile kept his head down as the guys from Sleeper Cell burst out laughing.

"That's what we should all do," said Adam. "There's nothing waiting for any us. Well, maybe him." He pointed to the most talented terrorist, who, like all the great ones, didn't seem at all surprised by the praise.

One of the other terrorists, with a sudden look of panic, asked, "What about me?"

"You're fucked. Everybody in here is fucked. So let's do it. Let's kill ourselves. Come on! Let's Hale-Bopp this shit right now!"

For a moment it was quiet.

"Hale-Bopp?" said Frankie.

"That cult down in San Diego," said Adam. "They all wore black Nikes."

"Just say Jonestown," said Ramon. "Everyone knows Jonestown."

Adam pushed open the door, but stopped when he heard Frankie yell his name. Adam turned around.

— 101 —

"Are you going to Del Taco?" he asked.

"No," said Adam.

Frankie pulled a twenty out of the register. "Bring back some tacos for everybody."

"Fuck that," said Adam.

When he got back to his apartment, Adam called a friend he hadn't seen in a while, a nice guy he knew from Long Beach State who now sold insurance. The friend sounded surprised to hear from Adam, but agreed to meet up. They got a drink in Santa Monica. "A few weeks ago I had to make a snack run to Smart & Final," Adam told him. "Guess who was behind me in line? M. Emmet Walsh!"

On Saturday Adam spent the day lounging in the pastel oblivion of Manhattan Beach. He drank margaritas at a fake dive bar and wandered up and down the terraced streets. He felt bad about his exit from El Goof, particularly the way he had talked to Frankie, but he didn't feel that bad. It was too nice just sitting there in the sand, listening to the waves.

He kept drinking when he got home. In a jolly mood, he ordered a pizza and finished off another season of *The X-Files*. He called his old friend to see if he wanted to come over, but he didn't hear back, so on his own he stumbled down to the video store to get the next season. The place was closed. He went home and passed out on the couch. However, the next morning, when his cell phone rang, he was no longer on the couch. Instead, he was facedown on the linoleum floor of his kitchenette. His phone read "Private," so he let it go to voice mail. Gray light seeped through the alley-side window. He sat up and rested against the cabinets. That's when he noticed the vomit, fanned across the floor and all over the front of his shirt. He had spent the night making vomit angels. The phone rang again and he answered.

"Why aren't you picking up?" said Max.

Adam rubbed his eyes. "I didn't recognize your number."

"The other day you hung up on me," said Max. "Did you think I had forgotten about that?"

"I waited for a long time. I figured—"

"I needed to talk, but you were gone."

"I'm sorry, Mr. Lavoy."

"I'm not saying you're a bad person. But, at the same time, I know that if I kept my feelings to myself, I would regret it. And honestly, just talking about it right now, I feel much better. There's probably no need for you to apologize, because as far as I'm concerned, that's all in the past. Are we okay?"

"Yes."

"Good. Because I need your help with something. I don't want you to panic, but this is kind of an emergency. I've already talked to Melanie and she cleared you for overtime. She said that's something you might be worried about."

"Okay."

"Leave now. And bring some towels."

Adam put his mouth under the kitchen tap and drank as much water as he could. As he threw his soiled clothes in the trash, he was thankful for his hangover. It gave him a kind of clarity, or tunnel vision, at least, that would be useful today and throughout his career with the show.

A half hour later, he rang the bell and took off his shoes, an old pair of New Balances. Max opened the door. He was wearing khaki shorts, a golf shirt, and a generic green baseball cap.

"You look terrible," Max said.

"I'm sorry."

"I'm not saying that to be rude. If I looked like that I'd want someone to tell me, so I could do something about it."

"I was sick last night," said Adam.

"Well, you're here. That's the important thing."

Adam, seeing that his Chuck Taylors were no longer on the rack, decided to carry his shoes as he followed Max into the living room.

"Sit down and I'll explain what's going on. Do you want a soft drink?"

"I'd love one," said Adam, taking a place on the couch.

Max crossed the room, but instead of going to the kitchen, he stopped at the giant window and peered into the canyon. "When I met my wife she was a beautiful and intelligent woman. This was a long time ago, when we were both at university. But then, over the years, she became a frump." He sighed. "For reasons I'm not eager to go into, she had our marriage annulled ten years ago. It was a complete travesty, of course, and since then I've been at odds with the archdiocese. I donated generously for many years, and I was a generous supporter of the new cathedral downtown. In fact, I made arrangements to have my bones buried in the crypt after I died, but not anymore. Not anymore." Max turned around, finally, and sat down on the edge of an ottoman. "Let's face it. I don't know you from Adam, so it's strange telling you all this. And maybe it's strange for you too. I hope you're not nervous."

"No, but I'm thirsty."

"Good, because there's nothing to be nervous about. This is the easiest thing in the world. My wife and I have joint custody of our dog. It sounds silly, but it's true. I'm sure you've heard people laughing about it at the office. Anyway, I'm supposed to get Misty on weekends. But Joanne, that's my wife, she's decided, once again, to make things difficult. She wouldn't let me see Misty this weekend. Don't ask me why. It's impossible to know what goes on inside her head. The point is I'm tired of dealing with that woman. Misty's an old dog and I don't want to lose any time with her." He looked at his watch. "Joanne's extremely lazy. She always goes to *noon* mass at St. Elisabeth's. That's in Van Nuys. Do you know Van Nuys?"

"Not really."

"Van Nuys is a shit hole," said Max, moving toward the front door. "There's no other way to describe it. But that's where she chooses to live. It pains me to see her living like that. Like a frump."

Adam followed him into the foyer. Max opened a closet and pulled out a leash.

"Twenty-five years in Los Angeles and I never got a driver's license," he said. "That might be my greatest accomplishment in life."

"What am I supposed to do?"

"Misty's in the backyard. You'll just walk back there and get her. Or climb the fence if the gate's locked. I'd do it myself but obviously I don't want to be seen."

"What's her address?"

"Misty's?"

"Your wife's."

"Don't worry about that. I'm going with you." Max put on a pair of sunglasses. "Misty's bladder gets erratic in new situations. That's why I asked you to bring towels. We'll park around the block and I'll wait for you in the car."

They turned left on Laurel Canyon and coasted down into the valley. Max put the passenger seat into an almost upright position, gripped his knees firmly, and with the windows down and the wind in his hair, he said, "So the point I was trying to make, before you hung up on me, was that you can draw a direct line from Ravaillac to Oswald."

"Where should I turn?"

Max pointed left. "The similarities are uncanny. Like Ravaillac, Oswald imagined that he was part of something bigger, but like everyone else he was just acting out his own psychotic crusade. And yet it's amazing to me what a single person can be responsible for. Both men changed the course of history. That's really the idea at the heart of my book, if I ever finish it. I'm not like Sonck. Everything came easy to him. He published a book every year, sometimes two, and most of them were brilliant. It's demoralizing to think what other men have accomplished."

"You've done well for yourself," said Adam. "You're way more famous than . . . Sonck."

"A hollow victory." Max snapped his fingers and pointed. Adam turned off Roscoe Boulevard and onto a residential street of stucco ranch houses.

"Vile," said Max.

"I grew up in a neighborhood just like this," said Adam.

"Misty might start barking. Just make sure you approach slowly. Give her a rub under the chin. She likes that."

They passed the house, making sure Joanne's car was gone, and then Adam parked at the end of the street.

"Don't rush her on the way back," said Max. "If she wants to stop and sniff something, that's her right."

On his way down the block, Adam walked over a fading hopscotch and passed an old woman who was sitting in a lawn chair in the shade of her open garage. The transistor radio in her lap was tuned to the Dodgers game. When he got to Joanne's house, he stood for a moment at the edge of the patchy front lawn. It was a nice little house, light blue with white aluminum awnings over the front windows. He opened the side gate without any fuss and walked around the house to the backyard, which was completely paved over except for a few weeds sprouting in the cracks. Everywhere he looked he saw piles of dog shit swarming with flies. There was a gazebo in one corner, filled with junk, and sections of the brown cinder-block wall behind it had crumbled during some previous earthquake. Misty was nowhere to be found. Adam called her name a few times. When he didn't hear anything, he walked to the back door, which had a doggy door. He kicked at the flap, to see if there was a locked panel behind it, but there wasn't. Without any further ceremony, he got down on his hands and knees and stuck his head through the flap.

"Misty!"

She was right in front of him, curled up in the laundry room. She lifted her head and immediately started barking. Adam wedged his right shoulder through the doggy door and reached up, looking for the knob. He unlocked it and pushed the door open. He moved slowly, as Max insisted, but Misty retreated from the laundry room, still barking, her claws clattering on the dusty wood floor. Adam lunged, but the floor was wet and he slipped backward, landing hard on his hip and elbow. Misty was still barking. Adam, realizing he had slipped in dog piss, sprang to his feet. He walked into the kitchen, where he immediately met the gaze of a red-haired woman in a black bathrobe. She was drinking coffee at a small table.

"Are you a messenger?" she asked, calmly, holding her coffee cup just under her lips.

Adam shook his head slowly; he was too nervous to speak. Behind her, on the wall, there was a giant bulletin board overflowing with yellow newspaper clippings. Misty, suddenly quiet, was sitting at her feet.

"Don't worry," she said. "You're not in trouble."

"I work for the show. I'm the new P.A."

"I guess Max burned his way through all the messengers." She took a sip of coffee. "Is he here?"

"He's waiting in my car."

She nodded quietly. Her hands were pale and freckled and Adam could see thick crescents of dirt under her nails. In front of her a pair of scissors was resting on a thick pile of newspapers from all over the world, with headlines written in several different languages. He saw a fly looping over a sink full of dishes.

"Did he tell you what happened last week?" she asked.

"No."

"He took Misty on a walk up in the canyon and she got sprayed by a skunk. So do you know what that man did? He had a cabdriver bring her back here. He must've paid the guy a fortune." She shook her head in disgust and then looked at Adam. "Are you okay?"

"I'm sorry," said Adam. "I'm not feeling well."

"Do you want something to drink?" Her expression remained calm and businesslike.

"That would be great," said Adam.

She got up, adjusted her robe, and walked over to the sink. She pulled a glass off the pile of dishes, rinsed it out, filled it, and handed the glass to Adam. A pair of reading glasses dangled from her neck; instead of a chain they were held fast by a grimy white shoelace. Adam, still smelling piss on his shorts, looked down at Misty, who seemed exhausted after all the excitement. She had trouble keeping her eyes open.

"Has Max told you about his book?" asked Joanne.

"Yeah, he's talked about it. A lot."

"That's what he'll do. He'll talk about it and talk about it. And he'll never finish it. Do you know why?"

Adam shook his head.

"Because then he wouldn't be able to talk about it anymore."

"I'm really sorry about all this," said Adam. "Max said you would be at mass."

She blew her nose on the sleeve of her robe. "I'm sure he did. This isn't the first time he's tried something like this."

"I'm sorry."

"Stop apologizing. I know you're just doing your job." She reached down and rubbed Misty behind the ears. "You can go out the front door. Tell Max I said hello."

On his way out, Adam saw more bulletin boards; they covered every wall of the living room, layer after layer of curled yellow clippings, creeping up the walls like ivy.

Adam took his time getting back to his car. When he climbed in, Max said, "Where's Misty?"

The glove compartment was open and several maps were strewn about Max's feet, unfolded.

"What's that smell?" said Max.

Adam reached for a towel and started wiping himself off.

"What happened?" Max said.

"Joanne was waiting for us," said Adam.

"Goddamn her." Max slapped the dashboard and lolled his head back in frustration. "That woman is a genius."

Adam started the car, but Max gripped him firmly by the wrist.

"What are you doing? You have to go back."

JIM GAVIN

"I can't go back in there."

"Remind her that you're acting within my legal rights."

"She just caught me breaking and entering."

Max let go of Adam's wrist. "Okay. Drive over to the house. We'll both go."

"No."

"You don't understand. She doesn't exercise Misty. The woman just sits there all day, doing nothing."

"She told me about the skunk."

"Listen. I've made mistakes in my life. I know that. But to have my life *annulled*? You will never understand that kind of pain."

"How much did you pay the cabdriver?"

"My whole life I've abided in the magisterium, and now it's being used against me. I haven't taken the sacraments in five years. What if I died right now?"

"Did you even hose her off?"

Max finally looked at him. "Of course I did. I did everything I could for that dog, within reason. Now let's go."

"I'm not going back."

"Drive!"

"Stop yelling. I have a headache."

"Drive!"

"Mr. Lavoy, will you please shut up? Please?"

On Monday morning, Melanie bought Adam lunch at the studio café and they ate outside in the courtyard. He asked her more about her acting days, and she told him a few good stories, including the time she auditioned for *The Rockford*

— 110 —

Files. She didn't get the part, but she met James Garner, who seemed like a very sweet and genuine man.

"Please put me down as a reference," she said later, picking through her salad. "You won't have trouble landing somewhere on the lot."

"Are you getting a temp?"

"Sure. For a little while."

Adam wanted to recommend the guy he used to temp with, but he couldn't remember his name. One of the casting offices was disgorging midgets. Melanie gave him a hug and went back to her office.

Adam dropped his badge off at the police station on Main Street and then walked to City Hall to collect his final paycheck. Melanie had arranged for him to get a generous severance. When he got back to the show's offices, Doug had the keys to the Benz and he gave him a ride to the parking structure. He wasn't wearing his mask.

"So what was she like?"

"Who?"

"Max's ex-wife."

"She's probably the most amazing person I've ever met," said Adam. He got out of the cart and shook Doug's hand.

"Good luck with *Paralegals.*"

"That's dead. My new project's called *Nurse Practitioners.*"

They agreed to meet for lunch in a couple weeks, but Adam knew it wouldn't happen. Doug was a busy man and, in spite of himself, he was a total pro. Adam knew this was the last time he'd ever set foot on the lot.

• • •

On Friday, he arrived early. Frankie was stoned out of his mind and had no real memory of Adam's ignoble speech from the week before.

"I got my hands on some truly evil shit from Vancouver," he explained, holding up a plastic baggie. "Sometimes you have to treat yourself."

Adam tried to apologize, but Frankie told him to forget it.

By seven o'clock most of the regulars had shown up. Chris Hobbs returned, wearing a porkpie hat, and Adam instantly hated him again, but not as much as before. Hobbs found Adam and sheepishly promised to repay him for dinner, as soon as he could. Adam sat down, taking his normal place among the terrorists. The pedophile was there, as weird and dauntless as ever, and Ramon and Trapper Keeper were there, and a bunch of new people. Adam had nothing prepared. His plan was to sit there all night, drinking and cheering and listening to all the other souls who, like him, depended on the incorruptible spirit of El Goof.

Illuminati

Uncle Ray called me from the ninth hole at Canyon Crest.

"Listen, Sean," he said. "I want to do you a favor. Me and Fig, we've been talking. We've got a story for you."

It was ten o'clock on Friday morning. I got out of bed and looked out the window. The sky was still gray. I usually tried to sleep late enough for the morning fog to burn off along the coast. Sometimes this meant sleeping past noon, but I was willing to do it. I hadn't talked to Ray in over a year.

"Your mom says the studio is giving you the runaround," he said.

"You two are talking?"

"I called her yesterday to wish her happy birthday."

"Her birthday was six months ago."

"Come meet me and Fig for lunch."

"Out there?"

"We're getting steaks at the Mission."

"You're buying?"

"Sean," he said. "Get cleaned up. We're going to tell you this story. You can put it in a movie."

"You're buying, right?"

"Yeah, me and Fig."

Eventually I found some long pants and got ready for the drive out to Riverside. When I stepped onto the second-floor landing, I spotted Mr. Nishihara, the landlord, down below in the courtyard, trying to fix the pump on the fountain. The stone cherubs were parched. I waited for him to take a break, but he just kept at it, so I popped the screen out of my bathroom window and jumped down onto a dumpster.

Minty was down in the alley, taking a shortcut back from the beach. With his board under his arm, he walked barefoot on the jagged asphalt, expertly sidestepping broken glass.

"It's a toilet out there today," he said, looking up at me. His wetsuit was peeled halfway down. I could see a rash spreading across his chest.

"I'm having steak for lunch."

"Nice!" he said, raising his fist in solidarity. He kept walking and for a while I stood there on the dumpster, watching him until he disappeared around the corner.

There were two empty cans of Tecate in my passenger seat. I swept them down to the floor. Then I started my car. Then I kind of spaced out and forgot that I had started it, and started it again. That's the worst sound in the world. A dead bottomless shriek, like a knife in a blender. For the first time in months I felt awake.

I was still driving around on a spare tire. The Triple-A guy who had assisted me said that as long as I drove under thirty-five miles per hour, the spare wouldn't give out. Not for a while, anyway. A couple weeks had passed and so far it had held up. There was no traffic and the freeway felt quiet and peaceful, like an empty church. Instead of saying a prayer, I rolled down the windows and listened to the wind. A few people honked at me to drive faster. When they passed, some of them noticed my spare, and they waved at me, trying to apologize. I waved back, as if to say, *No problem!*

Somewhere east of Yorba Linda the tire disintegrated. Triple-A got there fast, like they always do, and the guy replaced my spare with a spare spare that he had on his truck. It didn't cost me anything. He told me the same thing, about not driving over thirty-five, and then I watched him merge into the bright and hazy afternoon.

When I got to Riverside, I parked on a side street and walked toward the Mission Inn, a bizarre configuration of domes, turrets, and flying buttresses. Once a perennial retreat for oil tycoons and matinee idols, it was now a clubhouse for men like Uncle Ray, who had made a killing in the commercial irrigation business. He and Fig ate there a few times a week.

A black iron gate led to the atrium, where birds chirped and fountains bubbled. Passing through another gate into the hotel proper, I found myself in the same dim and mazy corridors I once ran through as a kid. Ray and his wife Holly had moved to Riverside in the early eighties. According to Ray, that's where the action was—"irrigation-wise." I loved going out there as a kid, climbing the giant rocks that littered his sprawling property, and then going for dinner at the Mission.

When I was in high school, we stopped coming to Riverside. Later I found out that Ray had loaned my mom some money, a lot of money, a great deal of money, actually, and he never let her forget this imperishable act of Christian charity. It wasn't the first time she had gone to him for help. Over the years my mom had come to the bitter conclusion that the only reason Ray loaned her money was because he knew she would never pay him back. Instead of breaking her thumbs like a loan shark, Ray did something worse: he made her feel guilty and small for being such a financial wreck. Now and then, tired of paying tribute to his generosity, she would tell him to go to hell and they wouldn't talk for a couple years. But then my mom would screw something up, drinking her way out of a job, falling back into debt, and she'd have no choice but to ask Ray for help. Ray once took me aside and said, "It's not your mom's fault. Some people understand money, and some people don't."

When I was a kid, Ray liked to roll twenty-dollar bills into tight little balls and bounce them off my head. To his credit he always let me keep the money. At the time I thought it was hilarious, and I still do. It was easy for my mom to portray Ray as the bad guy, but as I got older I got tired of her putting on the poormouth. Ray did care about her and he tried to help in the only way that made sense to him. I respected him for making his own way in the world. He came from nothing. I knew he had come from nothing, because at every opportunity, Ray would say, "I came from nothing." Plus he could tell a story and make people laugh. Not many people in the world can do that. Even when he and my mom were fighting, he could make her laugh, especially when they got drunk. Once he made her laugh so hard she fell backward over the couch, Jack Tripper–style, a scene he would often reenact whenever there was a couch available, and she would start laughing all over again. When I finished college he called once a year to offer me a job in the irrigation business. For a while, after I sold the script, he called more often, asking when it was going into production. He got a genuine kick out of having a nephew in show business. He had an exaggerated sense of my career, and to better track my movements around town, he got a subscription to *Variety*.

And now I could still smell his cologne, permanently embedded here, like the mosaic tiles, and I followed the scent all the way to the bar.

"Hey, muscles," he said, emerging from a crowd of middle-aged men wearing pastel golf shirts.

In my mind, Uncle Ray would always tower over me, the pink, splotchy Irish face looking down, giving me the business. But in reality I had him by six inches. I could see every capillary in his nose. He put a shot of Jameson in front of me.

"Health," he said.

"Thanks," I said.

"You're gonna shit yourself when you hear this story."

"I hope so. It was a long drive."

"How are you?"

"Hungry," I said.

"Your mom said she's done with her nursing thing."

"Just her LVN," I said.

"Does that mean salary?"

"Not yet."

"Well, it's a good start. Right?"

"She's working weird hours but she likes it."

"How's her new apartment?"

"It's nice," I said. "There's a pool."

"Her old place was a dump," he said. "I was always worried she'd get mugged."

He reached in his pocket and handed me a printed business check, made out to my mom, for a thousand dollars. The memo said: "Forklift Repair."

"Mind giving that to her?" he said.

"Is this why you got me out here?"

"No! I just figure every little bit helps, right?"

I put the check in my pocket. Ray asked what I was working on. As I gave my vague answers, he casually practiced his backswing with an imaginary driver. It was his signature move. When I had finished talking, he looked out on the imaginary fairway where he had hit his imaginary ball. "Shot three under today."

"How's Aunt Holly?"

"What?" He squinted at me for a moment, confused. Then he realized I was referring to his wife of thirty years. "Yeah. She's great. Drink this."

Two more shots appeared.

"Look at Fig!" Ray announced, drumming the bar. He pointed across the room. "He's posing for holy cards!"

Fig, to the seeming delight of several young waitresses, was balancing an empty pint glass on his forehead. He was a short, wiry man with a sunburned face. For the last half century his hair had been slicked into a pompadour. The waitresses smiled relentlessly. My mom used to work at a restaurant in downtown Long Beach, near the convention center, and after a long night collecting tips from boozy conventioneers, she would come home with that same miserable smile.

"When do we eat?" I asked.

"I want you to meet some people," said Ray. He put his arm around my shoulder and guided me toward the magic circle of men. One by one, I shook hands with the Illuminati.

Gus Lavelle, a general contractor who built houses in the high desert, said, "I've heard all about you."

"They call Gus the 'Inland Emperor,'" Ray said.

"Fuck off!" said Gus, in good cheer.

Then I met Jerry Tolliver, who owned a shipping company.

"Wait till you hear this story," Jerry said. "It literally gave me the chills."

"When can I see your movie?" Gus asked.

"Never," I said. "It's not getting made."

Jerry, sucking meat from a chicken wing, said, "How come they won't make it?"

I shrugged, affecting a look of martyrdom.

"But if it's good, I don't get why they won't make it. It's good, right?"

"It's genius," I said.

"It's all who you know," said Gus.

"Get in good with the schnozolas," Jerry advised. "Otherwise you're fucked."

"Once you write this thing," said Ray, "we can start talking to people."

"We?"

"It's our idea. Me and Fig."

"Quid pro quo," I said. "I'm going to etch that on your fucking tombstone."

"There's no Easter Bunny, baby," said Ray, laughing, as the hostess summoned us to the dining hall.

Two years ago, all my dumb ideas and tenuous connections came together. I sold a screenplay to a finance company that was working with a production company that was developing a project for a pair of comedians who had appeared in commercials for a popular men's body wash that wanted to distinguish their brand by underwriting a feature film in which the body wash somehow played a crucial role in the plot. At the time I was doing close-captioning for television. I could type ninety words per minute and I made $24,000 a year. At night I took screenwriting classes through a collge extension program and one of my instructors was nice enough to pass along my script to his manager, who liked it, or thought he could sell it, at least, and one thing led to another. My script had nothing to do with body wash, but everyone thought that was an easy fix. After it sold, I was acutely aware that something absurd had just happened to me and I felt obliged to mock myself and the shadowy figures who had lowered the drawbridge on my behalf, letting me into the castle. The day I signed the papers I told the head of development an anecdote about Flaubert. I told him that as Flaubert was nearing the end of *Madame Bovary*, he wrote in a letter to a friend that he could actually hear the rhythm of the final chapters, the fall of every phrase, though he didn't yet have the words. I explained that I had experienced something similar as I approached the third act of my multiethnic buddy cop adventure comedy, *Hyde & Sikh*.

I planned this in advance, thinking it would be funny and convey some sense of proportion to the proceedings. But then the head of development, bright, sincere, handsome, looked at me with sudden admiration and asked which translation I preferred.

"Of *Madame Bovary*?" I said slowly, trying to buy some time.

I said I wasn't sure, which was nonsense, because I had only read one version. I never paid attention to things like that. I had ripped the anecdote from the intro to whatever edition I had. I looked at the young man sitting behind his glass desk. Who was this gorgeously literate sociopath?

"It's a tricky business, translation," he said dreamily, as he walked me to the door. I thanked him for the opportunity he had given me.

After taxes, and after my manager and lawyer got their piece, I took home $57,000, a figure that somehow was both less than I imagined and more than I ever dreamed possible.

I took my mom out to El Torito and told her the good news. I told her I had money, lots of money, a great deal of money. This was the happiest moment of my life. I paid off my student loans and a good chunk of my mom's credit cards. I still had about twenty-five grand, free and clear, and according to my calculations, this would last forever. I moved to Redondo Beach, a few blocks from the water, and I quit my job. Over the course of the next six months, I took meetings with a few production companies—"What worlds do you want to explore?"—and I spent the remainder of my afternoons kicking around the beach like a bona fide asshole.

Then nothing happened. The finance company dissolved, the production company lost their studio deal, and so forth. Nothing always happens. The literature of Hollywood is depressingly consistent on this point. During my brief period of decadence, I tried to remind myself that the fun probably wouldn't last, that all good fortune is prelude to disaster, and soon I would be starting over at a temp agency, trying to raise my scores on the Excel test. I tried very hard to remind myself that I was a fool, that the definition of a fool is anyone who thinks he is not a fool, but my weekends grew brighter and more expansive and I felt increasingly worthy of the exalted visions I had of my future, which for reasons I still don't understand, always involved sitting next to one of those "zero horizon" pools that seem to blend into the ocean.

We sat beneath an enormous painting of Teddy Roosevelt and his Rough Riders, charging up San Juan Hill. The dining hall was quiet and dimly lit. In this prosperous gloom, Ray listened with impatience to the wine steward.

"Just bring us a bottle of dago red," he said, slapping shut the leather-bound menu.

Fig buttered every piece of bread in the basket. His mouth was stuffed. He had a scar on his chin and a big gold ring on his right pinkie. Fig served with Ray in Korea. Once their superiors found out they were both scratch golfers—Ray had actually led El Camino College to a California state title—they spent most of their tours getting flown to Japan to play golf with generals. I had known Fig all my life. He'd show up with Ray at my birthdays and Little League games, but after so many years I still wasn't sure of his full name and I had no idea what role he played in this world beyond that of Ray's eternal golf buddy. I always assumed he was in the irrigation business.

"Look at this beauty eat," said Ray, amused. "His thyroid is out of control."

Fig gave him the finger and kept chewing. The waiter poured our wine.

"So listen to this. Last week me and Fig went to Santa Anita."

Another waiter brought our appetizers. I sipped my wine and settled in.

"There's a nice restaurant up on the terrace. I know everybody there. It's nice, we get a table by the window, watch the races, hit the buffet."

"Nice," I said.

"Fig likes a trifecta. So we talk to some of our guys and start going through the book. There's no doubt on the first horse, everyone's agreed on that. Pretty much the same for the second, but maybe a little more iffy. Fig calls up his guy and gets a little more out of him, so we feel okay. But the third horse, we have no fucking clue. A day at the races, right? Now Fig's hungry, if you can believe it, so he goes up to the buffet and I'm sitting there going through the book. I'm sitting there and Fig comes back with a roast beef sandwich. He's upset. 'What's the matter?' I ask him. 'Look at this,' he says, 'look what they did to the fucking thing.' He opens up his sandwich. It's just swimming in mayonnaise."

Fig, piling steak tartar on his buttered bread, shook his head in disgust at the memory.

Ray continued. "This is a problem, the mayonnaise. There's no reason to just slap it on like that. 'What I would like,' Fig says, 'is just a cup of mayo on the side. So I can put it on myself.' Which is totally rational. Who wants that much mayonnaise? Why should some guy making a sandwich get to decide how much mayonnaise you get? It's tyrannical, if you think about it."

Ray paused to let me think about it.

"I tell Fig, 'You should've just asked for a side of mayo.' 'I know,' he says, 'but the guy was already making it.' I grabbed the maître d' and I told him the situation. 'Listen. Bring us another sandwich, but have your guy put the mayo on the side. I mean, for the love of all that's holy and merciful, bring us a side of fucking mayo!'"

Fig looked at Ray. Their faces were turning bright red.

"So here it comes. Roast beef, open-faced, and a big cup of mayo. Victory is ours."

"Well done," I said.

"But here's the thing," Ray said.

"I figured there was a thing."

"I go back to the book. I go back to pick the third horse for the trifecta. I look down the page. And there he is, right there at the bottom—*Side of Mayo!*"

Ray poured his wine to the top of the glass. He took a sip

and then pounded his fist on the table. "We both took home ten grand! Well, give or take. Can you believe that?"

There was silence. Ray, as always, had taken over the room. At other tables men were grinning and hanging on his every drunken word. Alcohol, for Ray, was a kind of charm, allowing him to barge through doors and announce his place in the world. Over the years he had diligently boozed and golfed his way to the top. This path to glory belonged exclusively to men. My mom could drink most men under the table, but her talent was considered grim and unsightly; instead of opening doors, alcohol isolated her, and no matter how hard she tried she was never able to drink her way into the magic circle.

"It's a good story," I said, finally. "But . . ."

"What do you mean, 'but'?"

"I wouldn't really know what to do with it. At this point it's just an anecdote."

Ray squinted at me. "What the hell are you talking about?"

"I mean, characterwise there's definitely something."

Ray and Fig both looked confused.

"That wasn't the story," said Ray.

"It wasn't?"

"Fuck, no!" Now they were laughing. "Who'd want to see a movie about me and Fig?"

"Okay," I said, "what's your story?"

Ray nodded gravely at Fig, who finished chewing and carefully wiped his mouth with the linen napkin.

"There's this alien," he said, and looked nervously at Ray.

"Go on, tell him."

"There's this alien. And what he does is come here, to earth, to hunt humans."

Fig, sweaty and exhausted, sat back in his chair.

"The way humans hunt deer," Ray explained. "You know, for sport."

In front of me there was a plate full of bacon-wrapped shrimp. I ate one and said, "That's *Predator*."

"What?"

"*Predator*, with Schwarznegger. You're describing *Predator*."

Fig was devastated. He dropped his head and began to massage the loose cartilage in his nose. I gathered that one of them had recently watched *Predator* on cable in a drunken haze, totally forgetting about it until this morning, when the dim memory surfaced as an idea of their own. Ray wasn't giving up.

"It doesn't have to be an alien," he said. "It could just be some crazy guy who hunts humans for sport."

"That's *The Most Dangerous Game*," I said.

"Well, Christ, it's all the same cha-cha," said Ray. "We can come up with something else."

My steak was unbearably delicious. We stayed in the dining hall for a couple hours, getting drunk, throwing out story ideas, and discussing the possibilities of studio financing. Ray, who had been installing sprinkler systems for the last thirty years, seemed to know way more about the process than I did. On our way out we filed into the men's room. My uncle and his buddy Fig belonged to that vanishing breed of men who piss with their hands on their hips. In another age such confident figures would've been immortalized in stone.

As the valet brought around Ray's Cadillac, Fig pulled a flask out of his pocket and took a sip. Suddenly, he put a hand on my shoulder.

"You've always been like a son to me," he said.

I laughed. "*Son?*"

Fig dropped his eyes in embarrassment. "I'm sorry, Sean. I'm just really proud of you."

He climbed into the backseat of the Cadillac and lay down. Ray yawned, handed the valet a twenty, and got in the car.

"We'll talk!" he shouted over the revving engine.

I had a parking ticket when I got back to my car. It was almost four o'clock. I got lost going to the freeway and ended up following the train tracks west for a few miles. I came to a beaten down section of Riverside where every block had the same rhythm. Auto body shop, tattoo parlor, bail bonds, checks cashing. The sidewalks were empty but for one guy, a twitchy, shirtless maniac wearing camouflage pants. He had a garden hose coiled over his shoulder and he kept turning around quickly, again and again, like he expected to catch someone following him.

On the way home, I decided to stop by my mom's new place in Buena Park. I got stuck in traffic on the 91, which gave me time to sober up. I inched along for an hour and finally pulled off the freeway. The front door of her apartment was surrounded by empty clay pots. She brought the pots with her every time she moved, saying she was going to fill them with dahlias and marigolds, but she never did. I knocked but she wasn't home, and her cell phone went right to voice mail. She probably had an evening shift. The stucco walls were cracked and peeling and the pool in the courtyard was full of leaves. I tore up Ray's check, scattered the pieces in the water, and sat down on a lounge chair. I knew it would be a long time before she got home, but I was willing to wait.

O mother, save me from the wisdom of men.

Bewildered Decisions
in Times of Mercantile Terror

B obby's office, for the time being, was the Berkeley Public Library. On a Thursday afternoon in August, with sunlight pouring through the arched windows of the reading room, he closed his book and quietly observed the homeless man sitting across from him. The man was bald and sunburned and he had grimy strips of duct tape wrapped around his fingertips. With a chewed-up pencil in his hand, he scrawled notes in the margins of an old physics textbook that was crawling with ants. Bobby couldn't take his eyes off the ants; he watched them moving in clusters across equations and diagrams, and it occurred to him that the ants were messengers, reading the book for this infernal professor, and when they were done they would crawl up the man's arm and into his ear, burrowing directly into his brain.

Bobby hadn't slept in two or three days.

He looked around for another table, but the reading room was packed with the elderly and the unemployed. Some people seemed hard at work, or at least pleasantly engaged, but most were either asleep or staring out the windows, as if waiting for something. It felt more like a bus terminal than a library. Bobby wore a Cal T-shirt and a pair of board shorts. He was trying to read a reference manual on patent law, but it was boring and his eyes kept slipping off the page. The hours were melting together. Last night, after *Conan*, he had fallen into a vortex of infomercials and then, at some point, he snuck off with his roommate's laptop and sent another pleading email to Nora, his dearest cousin and benefactor. When the sun came up, he left his apartment in the Berkeley flats and rode his bike up University Avenue. He ate breakfast at McDonald's and when he got to the library at nine o'clock, a crowd was already waiting to get inside. He struggled with his work all day—he kept taking long breaks to read magazines—but his lack of concentration, he knew, had more to do with excitement than fatigue. If anything, he worried that he was too awake.

It was three o'clock. Far up the hill, on campus, the tower bells were ringing. Bobby closed his eyes and listened. As a student, he had always loved the swirling bronze melody of the carillon. Ten years ago he had gone to Cal on a swimming scholarship. He majored in business, pledged a fraternity, and flunked out his junior year.

"See you later," he said, standing up and collecting his things, but the homeless man ignored him. In his own pungent way, this guy was a snob, and Bobby could respect that. It was a snobbery well earned. When he died alone in a gutter, in a puddle of his own piss, he would take with him a crazed and singular form of expertise. Bobby ran his fingers through his buzz cut. He wished he had a nice hat to doff, a bowler cap or fedora. He hated belonging to such a crude and hatless generation.

He sat down at a computer. His Yahoo mailbox was filled almost exclusively with undeleted spam. Someday, Bobby imagined, a single pill would grow hair, restore virility, and consolidate debt, but until then the market was wide open and he still had a chance to capitalize on his terrible idea. With this in mind, he scrolled down and was relieved to find a response from Nora. He had been trying to reach her all week, to get her advice on how he should go about branding the Man Handle, but she wouldn't answer her phone or reply to his emails. This happened sometimes. She was director of marketing for a company that sold investment management software. When she was on the road, she closed ranks and forgot about everybody in her life who wasn't a client or prospect. He would go weeks without hearing from her. Then she would come back to the city, haggard and lonely and claiming that she was sick of her job, that she was ready to meet a decent man and go into full suburban lockdown. Nora was tall and pale and, because of her pixie haircut and listless expression, men often asked her if she was a model. She had actually paid her way through college doing catalogue work, posing in cardigans next to duck ponds, but she liked to tell potential suitors that she was dying of consumption. Bobby and Nora had always been allied by a certain ghoulishness. At his father's funeral, when they were both seniors in high school, she met him on the front steps of St. Bonaventure in Huntington Beach and said, "Your eulogy sucked." They rode together from the church, passing a bottle of Jameson back and forth, and when they got to the grave site Nora took off her heels and ran across the expansive lawn, scattering crows like a burst of black confetti.

Now and then she met a guy who appreciated these qualities in her, but it would never last. They either got frustrated with the demands of her career, or she got bored with them. Bobby despised most of the men she dated. She had a weakness for solvent hipsters—architects, creative directors at advertising agencies, and other lieutenants in the corduroy mafia. They all supported progressive causes, not in any active or financial way, but just in general, as a kind of ambience that made them feel good about themselves as they walked around the city in vintage Japanese tennis shoes. And yet, in some ways, Bobby understood the plight of these slender prince-lings. Nora had a unique gift for turning cold on people.

The last time he saw her was three months ago, in May, when she asked him to accompany her to Geneva Software's annual Client Appreciation Party. The latest staff restructur-ing had left the marketing and direct sales teams looking grim and sparse, so her boss, Dave Grant, Executive Vice President and General Manager of Global Accounts, had encouraged the survivors to bring a guest, because the clients would feel more at ease in a full room. "There's free food for you," Nora told Bobby. "Just look presentable and keep me entertained." He got a haircut, wore a gray suit that he found in one of his room-mate's closets, and in a hotel bar overlooking Union Square he shook hands with Nora's colleagues, mostly men, who seemed weirdly impressed by the fact that Bobby was stuck doing plumbing work. He used to work summers with his dad, doing repair and remodel jobs, so he knew what he was doing most of the time, but he didn't have a license and he was getting paid under the table by a shady house flipper in Castro Valley who had posted an ad on Craigslist. But still, the men from Geneva software expressed wonder and delight, as if they were shaking hands with a sea captain or gunslinger. When Bobby asked what they did, most seemed vaguely ashamed that they were marketing associates or software engineers; in parting, they all shook his hand with a substantially firmer grip.

Nora introduced him to Dave Grant, who, despite being the boss, seemed nervous and fumbling around her. "That fucker's in love with you," said Bobby, as soon as Dave left, and Nora feigned vomiting. They were having a great time. Someone handed Bobby a drink; someone else, mistaking him for a client, handed him a gift bag filled with coffee mugs and key chains emblazoned with the Geneva logo. He watched a stray red balloon wedge itself in the crystal arm of a chandelier. Bobby told Nora that he wanted a job with her company—"I have sales experience," he reminded her, crushing a lime into his vodka—but then one of her company's actual clients found her and said hello. Nora turned her back on Bobby and began speaking in tongues. Bobby heard the word "functionality" repeated over and over. She made no attempt to introduce Bobby and for a long time he hovered awkwardly behind her, feeling invisible. When the client finally left, she turned around like nothing had happened. Later, in the cab, Bobby screamed at her, "You *literally* turned your back on me."

"It was client appreciation night, not Bobby appreciation night," said Nora, offering him a sip from the bottle of champagne she had stolen on the way out. When they stopped at a light, he grabbed the champagne bottle and threw it out the window. It smashed against the curb and for a moment they both sat there in silence; then Bobby jumped out of the cab.

He hated Nora for a couple weeks, but kept hoping for her to call and apologize to him. When his cell phone got shut off, he checked his email obsessively, but there was nothing. Since they were kids, growing up a few blocks from each other, they had always fought and made up, and the time in between was pure desolation. But he never heard from her and he realized that he was being overly sensitive and a little self-righteous.

He envied Nora's ability to turn herself on and off, to indulge in vile misanthropy one minute and false pleasantry the next. This golden switch guaranteed her future. She had a great place in the Inner Richmond, and on more than one occasion she had loaned money to her dearest cousin, though both knew it was a donation. She had worked hard to establish her place in the world, while he had made a shambles of his education and drifted from one crappy job to the next. He didn't have the on/off switch, and he understood now, with thrilling clarity, that Nora's path to success—corporate, dignified, incremental—would never work for him. Bobby required a bonanza.

In the email he sent last night, or early this morning, he told her he would be in the city tonight, ready to show her the prototype. He encouraged her, only half joking, to bring along some of her venture capital friends. The Man Handle, he explained, would appeal to the very men who had the power to invest in it. Indeed, it was a tool that no depraved capitalist could do without. He sketched out his business plan, which had evolved over the last few days from a few bullet points of satirical bombast to something that actually seemed plausible and real, and then he took some time to tell her how things had been going for him, personally, since they last spoke that night in the cab. In June, the house flipper had disappeared, without paying Bobby for his last month of work. After that he answered a Craigslist ad—"$$$$ Sales Pros Needed $$$$"— and got hired to sell ad space for an East Bay newspaper conglomerate. It was horrible and he discovered, once again, how much he hated sales. At some point he stopped going to work and by now he was pretty sure they had fired him. He was broke and the walls were closing in, but in this moment of darkness, he had found inspiration. Cometh the Hour,

Cometh the Man Handle: the thing pretty much marketed itself. However, his sudden lack of income and increase in free time was causing friction with his latest batch of roommates. The guy farthest down the hall, a programmer from Lahore, had caught Bobby using his laptop a few times, and Bobby knew that it was only a matter of time before the guy slit his throat with a bejeweled dagger. Looking back, it was a pretty macabre email and it worried Bobby that her response was so short. Nora usually wrote back in a tone and style that was as equally paranoid and macabre, but this time she just said that if he was around, she could meet him for a drink in the city at eight o'clock, and she named her favorite Irish pub. Even worse, she had signed her name without the usual "love" or "cheers" above it.

As he left the library, the alarm went off. A security guard asked to see his duffel bag. Bobby complied and watched the guard remove a book.

"I forgot to check it out," Bobby admitted.

The guard then pulled out a twelve-inch length of brass pipe that had been wrapped in black grip tape, the kind that went on skateboards.

"What's this?" he asked.

"It's a prototype."

"Of what?"

"The dumbest thing ever invented."

Bobby grabbed the bag from the guard and brought his book to the front desk.

"Please get in line," said the young librarian, a cute and supremely archetypal librarian—shy, bespeckled, and wearing a green cardigan, the kind Nora used to model. Bobby had wanted to talk to this librarian for the last couple weeks, but it seemed that whenever he had a book to check out, the desk was occupied by some miserable crone who would give him grief about his fines. Now, with a clear-cut opportunity, Bobby felt suddenly embarrassed by his appearance; he wished he had shaved, but all of his roommates' razor blades were dull.

The librarian stood a few feet back from the desk.

"This will only take a minute," said Bobby, putting his book on the counter.

"You can't check out reference books," said the librarian.

"Just me, or everybody?"

"Everybody."

"I'm joking!" Bobby handed her the book. "What's your name?"

"Catherine."

"I'm Bobby."

She nodded, and Bobby felt good when he got outside. He finally knew her name, at least. In the distance he could hear the final movement of the carillon. Before he got on his bike, he turned back to the library, a block of dusty green marble reposing in the milky afternoon light. It looked like the palace of a Babylonian king.

Earlier that morning, on her flight back from Los Angeles, Nora examined a laminated safety card that depicted plucky cartoon figures surviving a series of airborne catastrophes. Whenever she got on a plane, some part of her hoped for a crash landing. She was interested in her own reaction to mortal danger—would she act stoically or just shit herself?—but more than anything she thought about how fun it would be, afterward, going down one of those big yellow inflatable slides.

They were somewhere over the central coast. She could see brown hills, the ruffle of breaking waves. A few clouds dotted the sky, but otherwise it would be a pure blue drop. Members of the Geneva marketing team were spread throughout the cabin, sipping coffee and cooing into the bonnets of their laptops. In the next seat, Nora's assistant Jill scrolled through her iPod. Nora ordered a gin and tonic and when the drink came she asked the stewardess if she ever had the chance to go down the rescue slide.

"No," whispered the stewardess, a cheerful older woman with gorgeous silver hair. "And I hope I never do."

Then she patted Nora on the shoulder and, feeling her touch, the touch of a stranger, Nora almost melted with gratitude. She wanted to follow the stewardess down the aisle and sit with her on the jump seats. She wanted to ask for a job application.

This year's CTI Media B2B Software Development Conference & Expo had been, as Nora had feared, a brutal dry hump. Geneva had dropped ten grand for their booth, five grand for collateral inserts in the official conference backpacks, fifteen grand to have the Geneva logo placed on water coolers and cups spread throughout the exhibit hall, and twenty-five grand to sponsor a luncheon that featured, as entertainment, a sullen stand-up performance by a former cast member of *Saturday Night Live*. The carpet-bombing strategy had come down from Dave Grant, and with another staff restructuring on the way, Nora had asked him how he could justify this kind of spending. Dave felt confident that the risk would pay off, not so much in the short term, for staff, but down the road, for the company. "I'm sorry," he said, "but that's the reality of the situation." He showed some discretion, however, by staying in San Francisco and sending Nora to Los Angeles to handle the conference. That way, when she came back with a meager list of new prospects to hand over to sales, her name would be tarnished, not his. It was a suicide mission. Nora, who had always taken great comfort in the endless sorrow of Irish history, thought of De Valera sending Michael Collins to sign the Anglo-Irish Treaty.

For three days the pipe-and-curtain corridors were empty; the only people she really talked to were other software exhibitors. The asset managers and hedge fund reps who did show up to sample the goods were greeted as liberators; they nodded their heads, shook hands, exchanged cards, and left each booth laden with spoil. Yesterday was especially bleak and after packing up their booth the Geneva marketing team ran up a huge tab at a trendy tapas bar. Nora considered tapas a scam, so she left early and walked by herself through the barren maze of downtown Los Angeles. Part of her was hoping to get mugged—a major trauma would simplify everything. Her responsibilities, though dreary and minor, were all-consuming, and a nonfatal stab wound seemed like just the thing to get people off her back for a while. She hailed a cab and instructed the driver to take her to the nearest Del Taco, which was the only thing she missed about SoCal. At the Bonaventure Hotel she ate her No. 6 combo in a concrete alcove above the main lobby and then spent an hour riding the glass elevators, feeling more relaxed than she had all week. Later, curled happily in bed, with a full stomach, she turned off her BlackBerry and finished rereading O'Flaherty's *Famine*.

"Are you okay?" Jill asked.

"Yes."

"You're just staring out the window."

"I can see the ocean."

"If you're bored," she said, offering her iPod, "I have some NPR podcasts."

"I'm not a Bolshevik."

Jill laughed mechanically, and reinserted her earbuds. She had no time for the curdled sarcasm of her elders; whenever she laughed, it seemed like a calculated decision. A year removed from Stanford undergrad, Jill embodied the kind of blond forthright striving that Nora associated with Viking oarsmen. Her mind was keen and adaptive, streamlining every new project with speed and precision, but Nora had never quite trusted her assistant. She sensed that the girl had no experience with failure, at least not professionally. Nora amused herself with visions of what would happen after the next restructuring. Jill weeping at her desk; Jill throwing herself off the roof; Jill running amok with a shotgun. But these were only fantasies; in the end Jill would use her severance to travel through Asia or South America and then she would write about her experience in her business school application.

The plane landed safely and Nora and Jill got in a cab together. As they swerved onto the 101, Jill called her mom. She talked loudly and without embarrassment. Nora could never get over this—it was as if Jill and her mom were friends. Nora felt obliged, finally, to turn on her BlackBerry. It was only ten o'clock and she already had six emails from Dave Grant. There was a meeting at three o'clock in the "Golden Gate Room," which was actually just Conference Room B. Two years ago, when Dave became Executive Vice President and General Manager of Global Accounts, he renamed all the conference rooms after local landmarks. So far this was his greatest legacy.

She scrolled down farther and saw another message from

Bobby. She hadn't responded to anything he had written in the past week, even though she had been relieved to hear from him. He had a "business" idea, apparently, but she couldn't tell if it was a joke or not, which gave her a sinking feeling that she didn't want to deal with in the middle of the conference. Now, opening his latest message, the sinking feeling came back. The first paragraph didn't seem to end. She kept scrolling, and the paragraph went on for another three or four pages. Entire sections were set off in parentheses and she saw a distressing number of exclamation points. She went back to the top of the email and saw that he had sent it at four o'clock in the morning.

Bobby wasn't sleeping again.

They drove past Candlestick Park and through the gloomy hills of South San Francisco. The peninsula was shrouded in fog, but across the bay Nora could see the bright green hills of Berkeley and Oakland. He was somewhere over there, marauding in sunlight. She wrote back quickly, telling him she could meet for a drink. She would have to collect him. Get him drunk in a friendly atmosphere and then bring him back to her place and slip him a valium. It had worked before. Then she would call his mom, who was now remarried to a blackjack dealer and living in a trailer outside of Las Vegas. She would be very worried but in the end offer no real help. Nora's parents had always been there to bail out Bobby's parents—Bobby's father, an independent contractor, was a better plumber than businessman—and this arrangement had been passed down to the next generation. Six years ago, when Nora announced that she got her dream job in San Francisco, everyone on both sides of the family, instead of congratulating her, said with great relief, "You'll be near Bobby!" So now she would collect him, again, and then he would end up sleeping on her Pottery Barn couch for a month or two, eating all her food and generously offering to move in full-time, to help her out. The worst part was this: they would have a great time together, staying up late, watching crap on TV, and she would miss him when he was gone.

With a few hours to kill, Bobby decided to have a swim at the Claremont, a luxury hotel and country club in the Oakland hills. He rode his bike through campus and down Telegraph Avenue. He saw people on the sidewalk selling tie-dyed shirts, and he smelled vomit wafting down from People's Park. As a rule, he believed in the extermination of hippies, but here he was, ten years later, still hanging around Berkeley. After he flunked out of school, Bobby thought he would return to SoCal, but his mom wasn't there anymore, and neither were any of his high school friends. He kept trying to leave Berkeley, but then he would find a job or a new girlfriend. He paid cheap rent in the flats and he stayed in good shape riding his bike everywhere. Nora, on one of her rare visits to the East Bay, told him that he might as well learn how to play the sitar.

By the time he got across town and up the hill, he was soaked in sweat. He locked up his bike and took a path that led to the back of the hotel. Three years ago he got a job at the Claremont's poolside café. During his orientation, as he sat between two Senagalese nationals, the hotel's operations manager said that if anyone took more than fifteen minutes for their break, they were stealing from the hotel. Bobby actually liked the job. He walked around the pool all day, delivering gourmet sandwiches to hotel guests and club members. The sprawling patio offered panoramic views of the East Bay and on clear days you could see the Golden Gate Bridge. For a while he dated another server, who had just graduated from high school. One afternoon she stole a passkey from a maid and they fucked for fifteen minutes in the tower suite. In the fall, she left for college, and shortly after, Bobby got fired for stealing avocados from the kitchen.

Café employees used to take their smoke breaks on a balcony overlooking the tennis courts, but members complained and so management set aside a designated smoking area behind the hotel, next to the dumpsters. This was where Bobby found a high school kid in a café uniform. He asked him to get Salif, who, after three years, was still working as a cashier. "Tell him Bobby's here," he said. "We're old friends."

A few minutes later Salif arrived. He was fifty years old, tall and spindly, with yellow teeth and gray hair. Bobby once asked him what he did in Senegal before coming to the United States, and Salif told him that he had worked in a hotel.

"This is the last time," said Salif.

Bobby laughed. "You always say that."

At the pool gate, Salif told the guard that Bobby was a hotel guest who had lost his key card. They walked in together and Bobby threw himself on a lounge chair.

"I want an eggplant sandwich," he said, "and a glass of Chardonnay."

"Fuck you," said Salif in his sharp French accent.

It was warm and sunny, but across the bay Bobby could see fog rolling over the city. The guy in the next lounge chair was snoring. All around him women shuffled around in white robes, on their way to spa treatments. Bobby once bought Nora a treatment for her birthday—he got an employee discount—but when she came she ended up getting drunk in the hotel bar and never made it to her massage.

Bobby jumped into the water and for a long time he did an easy breast stroke, so he wouldn't splash anybody. He lost track of his laps. At some point, a bunch of kids dragged him into an epic game of Marco Polo. Volunteering to be all time "it," Bobby torpedoed through the crystal blue depths, hearing muffled screams on the surface. Every time he popped out of the water, he shouted, "Marco," as loud as he could. He could hear his voice echoing across the patio. The kids loved it and answered in kind. All his victims sat along the side of the pool, cheering on the last two kids in the water. Bobby trapped one of them in a corner, and then heard footsteps on the pavement. "Fish out of water!" he yelled, right before he heard a thud and a collective gasp. Opening his eyes, he saw a boy crying and holding his head. A few moms in white robes ran to him, and started calling for hotel staff. Bobby ducked underwater and swam to the other side of the pool. He grabbed his bag and left without drying off.

Coasting down Ashby Avenue, he kept seeing colorful flags out of the corner of his eye. It was like riding past a row of embassies, but when he turned to look, the flags were gone. At the BART station, Bobby walked to the end of the platform and stood by the tunnel, bracing himself for the rush of wind. Inside the train he concentrated on the BART map, its routes marked by elementary bars of red, yellow, and blue. It kept his mind off the black watery abyss waiting above him.

He got off at Powell, emerging into cold gray twilight. In his T-shirt and damp board shorts, he thought he might freeze to death waiting for the 38 bus, so he did jumping jacks until it arrived. He sat next to the window, looking down on Geary

Boulevard. At one stop, in the heart of the Tenderloin, an old drunk staggered up the steps and offered the driver a bouquet of dead transfers. The driver motioned for him to take a seat, but instead the guy walked down the aisle to the exit doors, threw his transfers in the air, and then hopped off. Bobby laughed but no one else on the bus seemed to notice the man's performance.

The pub was in the Richmond. It was nice and warm inside and the walls were decorated with portraits of poets and rebels. He had been here a few times before with Nora, who described it as "a proper pub." Now that she had money, Nora spent all of her vacations in Ireland, paying top dollar to recapture the glory of her family's destitution. It was her bizarro way of establishing legitimacy, like some derelict countess tracing her bloodline to an ancient king. Bobby didn't understand why someone who was born and raised in Southern California cared so much about a wet, miserable country she had no real connection to; but she always came back from her trips seeming refreshed, like she had gone home.

The girl tending bar looked underage. He asked if he could make a local call.

"I'll let you dial the number," he offered.

Her face was pale and freckled, like Nora's, and once again Bobby wished he had shaved. She handed him the portable phone and walked down to the other end of the bar. When Nora didn't answer her work phone, he quickly hung up and tried her cell. She didn't answer, so he left a message:

"Hey, it's Bobby. I hope you're having a proactive day, adding value and so forth. I'm at the bar. I got here early. I'm going to run a tab and let you pay for it when you get here. I'll probably need to stay at your place tonight. Also, my cell phone got turned off. And I need a new kidney. And the mob wants to kill me. And I've got the stigmata, again. Hurry up and get here."

He gave back the phone and asked for a menu.

"They're doing a pork chop tonight," the bartender said. She had an Irish accent.

"That sounds great. I'll start a tab."

"I can't run a tab without a credit card."

"Where in Ireland are you from?"

"A small place. You've never heard of it."

"I bet my cousin's been there. You two should talk. She'll be here soon. Do you know her? Nora Sullivan. She's in here a lot."

"I do know her," she said. "She always puts 'Fairytale of New York' on the jukebox."

"She said to go ahead and start a tab for her. She's on her way."

"I need a card."

Bobby handed her a credit card. "This one's expired, but just barely."

Her face was blank, but somehow a friendly blank. She took the card and he ordered a Guinness and pork chop.

A few men in the bar were wearing suits. One gentleman, grinning warmly at the bartender as he ordered a drink, had on a paisley tie and sharp-looking vest. In this den of brass and mahogany Bobby felt a sudden kinship, and once again he wished for a hat, something he could remove in their presence as a sign of respect. He pictured himself sitting in a top-floor office, with papers spread neatly before him awaiting his signature, and he saw on the far side of the polished table, cast in silhouette against the window, a row of faceless investors, nodding silently to each other, communicating annualized return rates through some sinister form of clairvoyance. Bobby was excited to shake hands with these fragrant and shadowy men. Once they felt the rugged texture of his hand, they would instantly understand the physical and psychological advantages provided by the Man Handle, and they would have no choice but to furnish Bobby with grotesque sums of money.

His pork chop was dry, but he enjoyed it, gristle and all, and then ordered another Guinness and a basket of fries. He finished those, ordered another Guinness, and at some point John, Paul, George, and Ringo walked through the front door. Four guys wearing Beatles wigs and dark, high-button suits. They were lugging instruments. Bobby called over to the bartender and she said it was Beatles night. A bunch of cover bands were going to play.

"Why are you making concessions to the British?" he asked.

"It's just some locals playing music."

"Why not a U2 night?"

"Because I'd fucking gag," she said, taking his empty glass.

In walked four Sgt. Peppers, arrayed in full Edwardian pomp.

"Who the fuck *are* these guys?" said Bobby, but the bartender was helping other customers. The pub was getting crowded. One of the mop-top Beatles, a short husky guy in his forties with a red, pockmarked nose, came up to the bar to order drinks. He had meaty hands and he was holding a scuffed pair of drumsticks.

"Ringo!" said Bobby, slapping him on the back.

Ringo looked startled, but then smiled.

"You guys are really going for it."

"That's what we do," said Ringo. "We always go for it on the second Thursday of every month." He tapped the brass bar rail with his sticks. "How's your night going?"

"Me?" Bobby was taken off guard. He couldn't remember the last time somebody had asked him a question about himself. "I'm meeting my cousin," he said. "She's late. It's already nine o'clock. I'm worried she's not coming. She's in here all the time. Do you know her?"

Bobby described Nora and as it turned out, Ringo did know her. He pointed across the bar to the band's John Lennon and said the poor guy had tried asking her out, without success.

"What's Lennon's day job?" Bobby asked.

"He doesn't have one at the moment."

"Then he doesn't have a chance," Bobby laughed. "Nora tries to slum, but she doesn't have the heart for it. She's going to marry somebody rich and boring."

"I thought she was very nice when I talked to her."

"I don't think she's coming."

"That's too bad."

"No, no! That's the thing. I should be in a bad mood, but I'm excited to hear you guys play."

"Are you a big Beatles fan?"

"Can you guys play 'Paperback Writer'?"

"We can definitely do that."

The bartender brought over four bottles of beer and Bobby, with a gallant flourish of his hand, indicated that this round was on him.

"I hope you guys had fun at the conference. I want to hear all about it, but first a few things. Now, keep in mind, this isn't me talking, this is everybody, and the reality is we need a backup strategy for wealth creation. From a solution standpoint, we need to execute right now, and the biggest problem I see is that we lack coordination in our pricing strategies."

Dave Grant picked up his juggle balls. Once they were in flight, he paced back and forth in front of a window that looked down on the bright streets of SoMa. The Geneva offices were next-door to the birthplace of Jack London. A plaque commemorated the site, and whenever Nora walked past it at lunch, she liked to imagine the old waterfront, a proper sink of iniquity, crawling with proper scoundrels and proper whores. She now sat on one side of the conference table, next to Jill and the rest of the marketing team. Mike LaBrocca, head of sales, sat on the other side of the table with his team, a pack of hyenas from third-tier MBA programs who spent their days quoting *Old School* and refreshing ESPN.com. A star-shaped conferencing unit at the center of the table transmitted the meeting to satellite offices in Chicago and New York. These people could hear Dave, but they couldn't watch him juggle. In spite of herself, Nora liked watching Dave juggle. It was soothing and hypnotic. He was only thirty-three years old, a wunderkind who decorated his office with memorabilia from his lacrosse days at Princeton and his stint in Guatemala with the Peace Corps. He spoke Spanish to the cleaning staff, expressing gratitude for their hard work. This made Nora want to vomit, and even more nauseating was the fact that most of the janitors seemed to genuinely like Dave, often seeking him out to say hello. They never said hello to her. Dave worked insane hours, sleeping a couple nights a week on the couch in his office, and yet somehow he made time to participate in a lot of expensive outdoor hobbies—kayaking, rock climbing, action kites. He had a nice tan and a nice family too; his wife and three boys were installed in a Noe Valley town house. One of his boys had survived leukemia, so on top of everything else, the fucker had overcome adversity and heart-break. Another star on his résumé.

"The question is, first and foremost, can you deliver? Or to put it another way, can *we* deliver? Either way, delivery is key. I want to emphasize that we're not being reactive here, just op-portunistic."

"I want to hear about the conference," said Mike.

"You bet. Nora can give us a rundown in a minute. But first I'd like to say a few things to get us started."

"Did you talk to anyone from Pinnacle Asset Manage-ment?" said Mike quickly, ignoring Dave. "I've been priming them for months."

"No," said Nora.

"So you guys basically went down to L.A., passed out some hats and water bottles, and then went to the beach."

"Pretty much. I spent the whole week snorting coke off George Clooney's ass."

"Okay, okay," said Dave with a nervous laugh. "Let's try not to have a tone here."

"Did you talk to *anybody*?" Mike continued, rising up in his chair. "I haven't heard a word from you guys all week."

"As a lover, George is both tender and thorough."

"That's great. Thanks, Nora. My guys are in the trenches all day, trying to sell—"

"*Trenches*? Is that a bar in the Marina?"

"No, I'm talking about actual trenches."

"Like World War I?"

"No, of course not," said Mike, rolling his eyes. "I don't mean *actual* trenches."

"Like *All Quiet on the Western Front*?"

"Look. I would never compare myself to a soldier. I have

too much respect for what those guys are going through with the wars and everything. I'm just saying that right now all the pressure's on us. On sales."

"There's a passage where one character is trapped down in the trenches and the only way he can get out is to take a knife and tunnel his way through the corpse of a dead comrade. He literally digs his way through the guy's intestines."

Dave put down his juggle balls.

"Mike, Nora. There's a lot of different ways to look at things, but we can't let a lack of clarity get in the way of our focus."

"Actually, Mike, I did talk to Pinnacle. Did you know they changed their name to the Randers Capital Group? Did you even know that? They want to upgrade their multicurrency capabilities."

"That's great," said Dave, "but going forward, our core challenges are still accuracy and efficiency. Are we accurate? Are we efficient? These are important questions, and from a business justification perspective you guys need to understand the role you play. Right now there's a disconnect between them and us about what 'commitment' means."

The room went quiet, and then Mike, with his eyes closed, said, "Who's 'them,' Dave?"

"Them is everyone. I know that sounds vague, but again, I'm not talking in specifics here."

"Let Nora talk. I want to hear about the conference."

"Who said that?"

"It's Gabe in Chicago. I want to hear about the conference."

"Hi, Gabe! While I'm thinking about it, I have a question on the finance side of things. And I'm throwing this out there to everyone, but mainly finance. What is the process in the event that cost basis information is not available when the action becomes effective? Do we get notified and reprocess internally or does the corporate action service prepare cancellation and rebook transactions to the blotter?"

"It goes both ways."

"Is that still you, Gabe?"

"Yes, it's me. It goes both ways. The door swings both ways."

Dave looked around the room. "What's so funny?"

"That's *Ghostbusters*," said one of the sales guys. "He's talking about Gozer the Gozerian."

"Who?" said Dave.

"John Belushi was supposed to be in that, but then he died," said a mysterious voice in either Chicago or New York. "Bill Murray took his place."

Another voice said, "Eddie Murphy was supposed to be in it, too. He was going to play the African-American guy."

"Winston Zeddemore."

Gabe's voice said, "So Nora was going to tell us about the conference."

"Let Nora talk," said several voices all at once.

"Listen," said Dave. "I know things are a little . . . right now. But still. We're trying to create a go-forward scenario, so we have to get out in front on this. We need confirmation on how our brand is being structured. And if we're serious about sustaining an effective solution environment, then we need to create a strategy for platform leveraging that prioritizes integration. That's the reality."

Nora's presentation didn't last long. She handed over a very small list of "promising potential prospects"—that's how she phrased it—and Mike and his sales team walked out in disgust. Afterward, Jill followed Nora back to her office. The brick corridors were dim and quiet. There wasn't a single phone ringing anywhere in the world.

"Are you okay?" Jill asked.

"Please stop asking me that."

"What's Mike's problem?"

"He needs prospects. That's our job."

"What about Randers?"

"Who?"

"The guys who used to be Pinnacle."

"I made that up. I wasn't going to let Mike ambush me like that."

Jill leaned against the doorframe. "I'm not sure that was the best idea."

"It doesn't matter. We're fucked."

"What do you mean? Do you know something?"

"Go call your mom," said Nora. "Tell her to fluff the pillows on your bed."

Jill looked at Nora with a sudden and superior calm. "I know you're upset right now, and I know you don't like me. But there's no reason for you to talk to me like that. It's totally unprofessional."

"Fuck off."

Nora's screen saver was a picture she had taken last winter in Ireland at the Cliffs of Moher. She went late in the day and had them all to herself, except for a group of young Russians, who hopped over the safety rail and pranced right along the edge, goofing around with each other, daring the wind to blow them into the ocean. A seven-hundred-foot drop, jagged rocks and crashing waves, but these Russians carried on, brave and merry in the face of death. She checked her email and in the minute that had passed since the meeting ended, Dave had managed to schedule another meeting with her at the end of the day.

There was a brief note from Bobby, saying he was excited to see her tonight. For a while she tried reading his previous email, the six-thousand-page epic. Parts of it made her laugh—what the hell was the Man Handle?—but most of it didn't make any sense. The worst part was that he seemed to know which parts didn't make any sense. She knew where this was going. The first time it happened, in college, campus security found him in the Life Sciences Building, throwing pine cones at the giant skeleton of the *Tyrannosaurus rex*. A couple of his fraternity brothers brought him to the emergency room. He told the doctors he couldn't sleep. His grades were terrible, his girlfriend had broken up with him, he didn't know what he wanted to do with his life . . . the same stuff everybody worries about, but he couldn't get a handle on it and everything snowballed. It happened again four years later, after he got fired from his hotel job. Nora saw this one coming. As his situation got worse, he became more and more cheerful, and his phone calls started coming later and later. She brought him to her apartment and got him to sleep, and later demanded that this time he get on some regular medications, or at least get some regular therapy. Bobby told her he was fine and for a couple years he was, but then he broke up with another girl, lost another job, and it happened all over again. He didn't have health insurance and Nora paid his emergency room bill. Three months ago, when he threw the champagne bottle out the window, she probably should've seen it coming, but even if she did she no longer felt any urgency to do anything about it.

She closed her office door, thinking she was about to cry.

But she didn't. Something rattled in her chest, but she didn't cry.

At six o'clock, she walked down to Dave's office. When he saw her at the door, he stopped juggling and reached for his jacket.

"Do you want to get out of here?"

They went down the street to a sports bar. The Giants were playing, so they had to fight their way through crowds moving toward the waterfront stadium. Dave kept looking back, as if he might lose her, and Nora realized she had never been alone with him. Here, in public, the veneer of dynamism fell away and he seemed pensive and unsure of himself. When he brought over their pitcher, he spilled some on the table, and got flustered as he looked for napkins.

"I'm sorry," he said, and carefully wiped down the table, sopping up every drop. He sat down, took a sip of beer, and Nora knew what he was going to say.

"At this point in time, Nora, we need to start thinking about migrating some of our resources to an outside vendor."

"Do I still have a job?"

"Yes! God, I'm sorry!" He almost spit out his beer. "I mean, that's the good news. For you, I mean. I'm not explaining this very well. Listen. We've decided to make some major . . . in a couple weeks. Direct mail, prospect management, customer analytics—we can't justify those costs right now."

"Are you leaving anything in-house?"

"Like I said, we can't justify—"

"Who's left?"

"You, mostly. The plan is to shift you into more of a liaison role with sales."

Nora leaned forward slowly and rested her forehead on the edge of the table.

"I want you to know that I fought for you and your team. But mostly you. That's why I wanted to maximize our profile at the conference. I was hoping something good might happen."

"That was a great plan, Dave. Thanks."

"I know this isn't ideal for you, but I did—I really fought for you."

"I heard you," she said, lifting her head, "and I said thanks."

"But you were being sarcastic. Which is okay. I understand. That's how some people cope with challenging situations. It's something I've always liked about you, the way you're kind of . . . everyone in the office enjoys your sense of humor. But listen. I fought for you and, going forward, I think you'll be in a good position. As Geneva evolves, you'll be right there with me, delivering the . . ." Dave stopped for a moment and stared at his beer. Finally, he cleared his throat. "Basically, the kind of mission-critical solutions that address the needs of our clients."

Outside the window a scalper was yelling and waving tickets. Nora asked in a sour tone if Geneva was going to sacrifice their luxury box at the ball park. Dave looked hurt, as if she had failed to understand something obvious, and said, "I fought for you."

Nora suddenly understood the evening's shape and direction. It was like floating on a river and hearing a waterfall in the distance. She signaled the waitress for another pitcher, and for the next hour she watched Dave get drunk. He couldn't handle his liquor, but that seemed part of whatever clumsy plan he had set in motion. By the time they got to the third pitcher, Dave was trying to pet Nora's arm. She lightly removed it and he looked ashamed. She got the feeling that he had never tried anything like this before. It was almost touching. Eventually his seduction devolved into a series of whimpering confessions about his family life and the pressures he was under at Geneva. He and his wife were constantly at odds, and he got the feeling that if the next restructuring didn't work out, he might get the ax himself.

"It's been a difficult time for me," he said.

Nora, still relatively sober, figured that if she offered him a choice, right now, between fucking her or crying like a little boy on her shoulder, he would choose to cry.

Dave paid the tab and they started walking toward Market, without any real destination in mind. At a crosswalk, he tried to kiss her, but she pushed him away. After effusive apologies, Dave reiterated that he was under a lot of pressure lately.

"I saw something the other day," he said, as they kept walking. "We took the boys to Golden Gate Park for a picnic. We're sitting there and a kid walks out of the bushes. She's a punk-looking kid. She could've been twelve years old or nineteen. I have no idea. But she's in ratty clothes and I swear to God she's got a homemade bow and arrow slung over one shoulder and a dead cat over the other. She walked right past us, like we weren't even there."

"I want another drink," said Nora.

Dave stepped away and made a phone call. They walked down Kearny and into North Beach. On the way, Nora's phone rang. It was Bobby. She let it go to voice mail and then listened to the message.

"What's so funny?" Dave asked.

"Nothing," she said, and when they finished their second round of cocktails at nine o'clock, she turned off her phone and said, "Let's get dinner."

• • •

"Next time Nora's in, she'll take care of it. I swear."

"It's fine. Do you want your credit card back?"

"No, keep it. As a token of my affection."

The barbacks were wiping down counters and turning off the lights. A fat Beatle was onstage, whistling to himself and unplugging his amps. Bobby picked up his bag and followed the bartender out the front door, where a few other Beatles were smoking. Ringo smiled and waved to Bobby.

Geary Boulevard was a cold, misty hollow, tilting toward the ocean. Bobby saw the bartender getting in a cab and ran after her.

"Where are you going?" he said.

"Home."

"You should stick around."

"Let go the door, you fuck!"

He heard voices behind him. A pair of John Lennons were moving toward him saying, "Hey, hey, hey . . ."

"Hold on," he said, turning back to her. "I want to show you my Man Handle."

He reached into his bag and she started to scream. Before he could show it to her, someone grabbed him around the waist. Bobby tumbled to the sidewalk. He watched the cab's red taillights disappear down the street. Slowly, the Fabs dispersed. Ringo helped him up.

"What the hell?" said Bobby.

"They thought you were about to do something."

"Do what?"

"Hit her."

"I'd never hit a pretty girl."

Bobby grabbed his bag and started walking down the sidewalk. Ringo caught up with him and asked if he was all right.

"Which way is the ocean?" Bobby asked. "I'm freezing out here."

"Do you want a ride?"

"Can you take me to Nora's house? It's around here somewhere."

As they turned and walked past the bar, one of Ringo's bandmates said, "What are you doing, man?"

"I'm giving him a ride."

"Tell him to take a cab."

"He bought us drinks all night."

Ringo had somehow packed his drum kit into the trunk of his Honda Civic. The trunk didn't close all the way, but he had everything secured with bungee chord.

"I'm glad Nora flaked," said Bobby, as they drove off. "I had a blast tonight. You guys are unbelievable. Where'd you get the wig?"

"It's not a wig."

"Bullshit!"

"It's not. I swear."

"Do you go to work like that?"

"I teach music. No one cares what I look like."

"That's lucky."

The avenues were washed out in an orange, syrupy light. It was like driving around inside a pharmacy bottle. All the houses looked the same. Bobby told Ringo to stop.

"I think this is it."

He rang the bell several times. Inside a dog started to bark, which was a bad sign, because Nora didn't have a dog. He heard footsteps in the hall and the door opened. Behind the metal security screen, an old woman in a bathrobe was looking at him.

"Who are you?" she said.

Bobby turned around and was glad to see Ringo still there, with the engine running. He ran down the steps and got back in the car.

"I thought that was it," Bobby said. He tried calling her with Ringo's cell phone. She didn't answer. They drove around some more, but Bobby had no idea where to go. BART had stopped running and so, without any other choice, he asked Ringo if he would mind driving him downtown, so he could catch the Transbay bus.

"I took it once a few years ago," said Bobby. "It was full of freaks."

Ringo puffed out his ruddy cheeks and tapped a beat on his steering wheel. Finally, he offered to let Bobby crash on his couch.

"You're a soft touch, Ringo," said Bobby. "That's what Nora says whenever she loans me money. She says, 'Lucky for you I'm a soft touch.'"

"My wife will be asleep," Ringo said. "So we have to be quiet."

They drove somewhere in the vicinity of Eddy and Divisadero and parked in the underground garage of a drab apartment building.

"What neighborhood is this?"

"I don't know. It's kind of a nonneighborhood. My wife calls it NoSo."

"What's that?"

"North of South."

"How long have you lived here?"

"Fifteen years."

When they entered his apartment, Ringo shushed him, and went down the hall to change out of his suit. The furniture looked dingy and secondhand, but the walls were resplendent with Beatles memorabilia. Ringo came back out in sweatpants and asked Bobby if he wanted some tea.

"Nora drinks tea," said Bobby absently, and walked over to the small strip of linoleum that marked off the kitchen. "Let me see your hands. Hold them out like this."

Ringo put out his hands and Bobby grabbed them. "Now, these are hands. This is what I'm talking about."

"What are you talking about?"

"There's texture here. Strength. Is that from drumming?"

"And guitar. I can play anything, really." Ringo dropped his head a little. "Jack of all, master of none. As they say."

"You look like a master to me."

Bobby grabbed his bag and handed Ringo the prototype. "This is the Man Handle. It gives your hands strength and texture."

"I don't get it," said Ringo.

"Right now it's just some pipe and grip tape. But when you're sitting around, doing nothing, you squeeze it and roll it in your hands. That's all. After a while you get calluses."

Ringo started to roll it in his hands. "Okay. But I still don't get it."

"We're going to market it toward managers and executives, so they don't feel bad when they shake hands with plumbers and other righteous members of the working class. It puts everybody on equal terms."

"Why would they feel bad?"

"I don't know. It's psychological. Bankers want to be cowboys."

The teapot whistled. Ringo made two cups and brought them over to the couch.

"It sounds dumb when I say it out loud," said Bobby.

"I don't think it's any dumber than half the infomercials I see."

"Thank you! The bigger the lie, right? Well, the dumber the idea, the more people will buy it. These are standard marketing concepts. What's your real name, anyway?"

"Alex. But my last name is actually Ringo."

"Bullshit!"

"Shhhh." Ringo showed him his driver's license. "You can't fight destiny."

Bobby picked up his tea and looked around the room. "Nora missed out. She should be here. Do you think something happened to her?"

"Are you worried?"

Bobby stood up and started pacing back and forth behind the couch.

"She was a fuckup in high school. She went to junior college and now she's making six figures." He sat down on the couch, and immediately got back up. "She hasn't been picking up her phone. I don't know if I should be worried. I think she's just mad at me. What part of town is this?"

"We can call the police," said Ringo. "If that would make you feel better."

Bobby sat back down. "No. I'm getting worked up over nothing. I had fun tonight. I've been talking and talking, but what about you? Are you good? Some of these guys Nora dates. They don't have any manners. They go on and on, and by the end of the night I know everything about them, and they don't know anything about me." Bobby looked out the window. "What floor are we on?"

"Third floor."

Ringo moved toward the hallway. He came back with a neatly folded blanket and placed it on the coffee table. "I'm going to bed. Will you be all right out here?"

"Don't go. There's probably something on TV."

Ringo declined with a polite smile and moved into the hall-way.

"Have you ever been in a fancy hotel lobby, with all the clocks set to different times around the world?"

Ringo didn't answer. There seemed to be some invisible force dragging him toward the shadows.

"All of us should hang out sometime," Bobby called after him.

He watched *SportsCenter* for a while, on mute, and then brought a chair to the window. He stared at a streetlamp far-ther down the street. He stared too hard and it flickered. All the streetlamps flickered, one by one. Bobby wondered how many units were in the building. He closed his eyes, trying to hear how many. But the place was silent.

Ants were crawling on the tiles above the kitchen sink. He looked through the cabinets, but couldn't find any snacks. Then he was standing in front of the bathroom mirror, shaving, first his face, and then his head. In college, he used to shave his head before every swim meet. He ran the razor through sticky mounds of Barbasol, giving himself little nicks on the top of the skull. Halfway through, he stopped and looked at himself. He suddenly wished he hadn't told Ringo about the Man Handle. It seemed to break the spell. Tomorrow he'd be back in the sunny East Bay, without any ideas. He wiped his head off and walked down the hall to the bedroom.

The door opened with a squeak and there was Ringo,

sleeping alone on a futon mattress. He was on his side, with his back to the door and a sheet pulled tightly to his chin.

"I can't sleep," said Bobby, walking into the room.

Ringo jerked awake. "What are you doing?"

"Scoot over, man," said Bobby. "I can't sleep."

Ringo tried to turn on a light, but Bobby jumped on the bed and knocked his hand away. Ringo rolled against the wall, with his back to Bobby. "Don't," he said weakly, covering his head.

Bobby slid toward Ringo and put his arms around him, burying his face in the back of Ringo's neck. For a long time they didn't move.

"Let me turn on the light," said Ringo finally, slinking down the bed. "Just for a second. Can I do that?"

"I can't sleep."

"I have something you can take."

"Don't go."

"I won't," he said, and the room filled with light.

Nora woke up right before her alarm went off. Halfway through her shower, she remembered that Dave was in the other room, sleeping peacefully on the couch. Only a few a hours ago he had announced, with a sense of triumph, that he couldn't go through with the act itself. Nora had shrugged and made coffee; then she listened to Dave talk about his family, the heartbreak and joy. "I'd be a fool to throw all that away," he'd said. She was impressed. By some miracle he had transformed the most despicable moment of his life into an opportunity to celebrate his own virtue. Now he would return home a better and more loving husband. Nora had fulfilled her role in his personal quest, just not in the way she had imagined—this chaste and redemptive version, somehow, was even more hollow—and he thanked her for understanding what he was going through. "I quit," she'd said, and for a while he tried meekly to talk her out of it, strongly advising her to wait for the next restructuring, so she could collect severance. "But I'm not getting laid off," she'd said, confused. "I thought I was moving to a liaison role with sales." Dave admitted that he hadn't totally worked out the specifics on that.

Later, in bed, she thought of Bobby swimming the butterfly, the way his head would pop out of the water in perfect rhythms, and the way he would suck in the air, as if every breath was going to be his last.

It was a bright gray morning. Nora finished dressing and came out to the front room. Dave had already left. The down comforter she had given him was piled on the floor between the couch and coffee table. She folded it and left for work.

Jill was waiting for her when she got out of the elevator. She was her normal chipper self, having already forgotten the horrible way Nora had treated her yesterday. Nora found this deeply annoying; she had no patience for people who didn't hold grudges.

"Are you okay?"

"I'm hung over."

"There's a funny-looking guy in your office."

She recognized him from Beatles night at the pub. It was absurd seeing him now, in this context. He wore jeans and a ratty fleece, but the mop top remained, crowning his pudgy red face.

"I'm Alex," he said. "Bobby's asleep at my place."

Somehow this made total sense. He drove her to his apartment. The car's ashtray was overflowing and he used T-shirts for seat covers.

"He thinks the world of you," he said.

"Why'd you take him back to your place?"

He looked at her as if he didn't quite understand the question. "He was stuck out here."

Back at the apartment, Alex warned her that Bobby had tried to shave his head. "Wonderful," she said. Alex made tea while Nora went to check on Bobby. When she sat at the edge of the bed, he looked at her with groggy eyes. He smiled and ran a finger along one his bald streaks.

"How do I look?"

"Come on," she said. "I'll fix it."

She brought him into the bathroom. He knelt in front of the sink, staring at himself, while she quietly shaved his head. He smelled like chlorine. When Nora finished, she sprayed a wad of cream into her hand and ran it through her hair.

"What are you doing?" said Bobby.

Nora didn't say anything. She just handed him the razor.

Middle Men

Part I: The Luau

As a boy, Matt Costello often wondered what his dad did when he left the house in the morning. The old man was in sales, he knew that, and from the brochures and catalogues stacked in the garage, he knew it had something to do with toilets. This always seemed like a joke to Matt—toilets!—and he didn't understand why anyone would choose to go into this line of work. Years later, while half-assing his way through college and trying to decide what to do with his life, he finally asked his dad how he got into the plumbing industry. The old man, with his usual modesty and good humor, explained that when he returned from Vietnam in 1969, his only goal in life was to work someplace with air-conditioning. To that end he answered a classified and got hired to work the order desk at a toilet warehouse somewhere in the industrial corridors of South Los Angeles. This decision led to a lifelong career as a plumbing salesman, a twist of fate that seemed funny to Matt, or did for a while, anyway, as he wasted away his twenties bartending, coaching soccer at his old high school, and not quite finishing his university education.

Then his mom got sick. Matt quit all his jobs, moved home to Anaheim, and spent the next year helping to take care of her while she endured chemotherapy. Several of his closest friends had lost their moms to cancer, so he knew the drill. This happened to everybody sooner or later, and he marveled at the quiet and dignified way his friends had moved on with their lives. He looked forward to doing the same, earning his credentials as a stoic and joining their club, but when his mom died, he failed to live up to their example. His mom was a fierce, deadpan woman, and deeply practical. Before the cancer got to her brain, she carefully planned her own funeral. She wanted "On Eagle's Wings" for the recessional hymn and she dispatched her daughters to JCPenney's to pick out a dress for the coffin. "Nothing too fancy," she said.

After she died, Matt, for his pain and loss, felt entitled to many rewards. He secretly anticipated, in no particular order, a moment of spiritual transcendence, the touch of a beautiful and understanding woman, and some kind of financial windfall. Instead, at thirty, he was broke and living at home. His sisters, the true stoics in the family, had both moved out and resumed their careers. The house was empty in the afternoons, so he sat by the pool and watched the water turn green. At night, when his dad went to bed, he'd load up on his mom's leftover Vicodin and watch *The Office* over and over. That bit in the Christmas special, when Tim says he'll get a drink with David Brent, crushed him every time.

Enough was enough. A month after the funeral, his dad talked to his boss, Jack Isahakian, of Ajax Plumbing Sales, and Jack offered Matt a job selling toilets. With no other prospects, he accepted. Now, a year later, deeply aware of his own vanity and foolishness, he was sitting through another sales meeting at the Ajax warehouse in Compton.

Larry Rembert, the factory guy from Brentford, paced back and forth in the dusty light of the wood-paneled conference room. Ajax repped Brentford toilets throughout SoCal. It was one of their glamour lines. Larry, a short, paunchy black man in his fifties, finished his third can of Budweiser and held up the new Brentford catalogue. He turned to a picture of the new vitreous china siphon jet urinals.

"The flushing velocity on these things," he said, "is fucking breathtaking."

Matt noticed all the veteran outside salesmen taking notes. Realizing he didn't have a pen, he sank down in his seat. At the front of the room, his father, Marty Costello, the top outside salesman at Ajax, tapped his fingers on his knees, jonesing for a cigarette.

Larry assured Jack that the improved pricing and rebates would strengthen their position with commercial contractors. On the residential side, he hyped the Ultima 900, an elongated vacuum-assist two-piece with a newly designed anti-siphon ballcock, and apologized, once again, for the old ballcock, which was recalled this past spring, causing chaos for new-work plumbers throughout Los Angeles, Orange County, and the Inland Empire.

Afterward, Larry repaired to the Panorama Lounge of the Holiday Inn in Long Beach, where, amid moody neon tube lights and smooth jazz renditions of contemporary pop hits, he bought drinks for all of Ajax's outside salesmen and for a group of aerospace engineers who had been laid off earlier in the afternoon. He rehashed key points from his recent speech at the Association of Independent Manufacturers' spring conference in Reno, and spoke with conviction on a variety of topics. He had his doubts about the war in Iraq ("Rumsfeld's a fag"), he worried about the state of the NBA ("all these Serbian dudes look like vampires"), and he loved the new season of *24* ("a total mind-fuck").

At some point in the evening, as Larry staggered around the bar, trying to make a case for the existence of the chupacabra ("I've seen some *things*, man"), Jack steered him toward Matt.

"This is Marty's kid," said Jack, standing between them. "He's our new bottom-feeder. Maybe you could ride with him tomorrow. Help him out."

"You bet," said Larry, and then, leaning in close to Jack, he whispered, "I'll take him to the luau."

For some reason, the word "luau" distressed Matt. He thought it might be code for a sadistic initiation rite known only to toilet salesmen. There was a lot of lingo in the industry and still, after a year, he barely understood what anyone was talking about. He wanted to ask for specifics, but Larry and Jack were busy ordering another round and his dad had already gone home.

At nine o'clock the next morning, Matt pulled his black Kia Spectra into the Holiday Inn parking lot. He called Larry's cell, but there was no answer, so he idled for ten minutes, listening to Jim Rome's opening segment. Another fifteen minutes passed. Badly hung over, Matt decided the only intelligent way to deal with the situation was to park somewhere and sleep.

— 168 —

Since getting hired, he averaged nearly six hours a day on the freeway, calling on wholesale plumbing accounts from Long Beach to Victorville. This constant and solitary pursuit, across landscapes bright, hazy, and inscrutable, had started to infect his dreams. When he fell asleep—on the couch, usually, in his Garden Grove apartment, after watching several hours of soccer and flipping through the softcore offerings on Cinemax—he saw nothing but empty freeways. His dream freeways were always thousands of feet in the air, higher than the tallest buildings downtown, and the transition loops were banked at impossibly steep angles. Now Matt found himself somewhere above the coast, among clouds, screaming across a vaulted tangle of concrete. His Spectra flew off the side and he felt himself falling, falling slowly, with great pleasure, into a vast and merciful ocean.

"Look alive, you fucking goldbrick!" Larry pounded on the window. "Open up!"

Matt wiped drool from his face and turned down the radio. As Larry opened the door, Matt cleared the mess that had been accumulating for weeks in his passenger seat: catalogues, price sheets, line cards, old newspapers, and countless bags of Del Taco.

Larry threw a briefcase in the backseat and climbed in. He was wearing pleated khaki slacks, a bright orange fanny pack, and a gray golf shirt embroidered with the logo of Brentford Plumbing, Inc., of Yuma, Arizona.

"No wonder Jack gives you all the dogshit accounts."

"Sorry. I'm pretty wrecked."

"Lightweight." Larry pulled out a canister of Binaca Blast, opened his mouth, and fired off several rounds. He pointed

— 169 —

toward the drab modern tower looming over Lakewood Boulevard. "These circular Holiday Inns fuck with my head. I couldn't find my room last night. I woke up in a stairwell."

"You can go back to bed if you want," said Matt.

"No, I just need some breakfast." Larry took a pack of Kools out of his fanny pack and lit one up. "I don't mind if I smoke. Do you?"

"Maybe you could just roll down the window a little," uttered Matt, hearing in his voice the same fatal note of politeness that doomed all his efforts as a salesman.

"You bet," said Larry.

They went to IHOP.

"I've been on the factory side for a while now," explained Larry, as he emptied a bottle of Tabasco on his omelet. "But before that I was in the rep business in L.A. for almost twenty years. Brass, china, tools, pumps. You name it, I sold it."

Haze poured through the window, illuminating the spotty silverware. Matt had to squint to see Larry, who seemed a blur in the morning light.

"How do you stand it living out there in Yuma?" asked Matt.

"It's hot," Larry said, "but there's no traffic and nobody hassles you. I can sit in my yard and shoot jackrabbits all day if I want. I can shoot other things too. Crazy things."

"Is there a lot of new construction out there?"

"Not like out here."

"I call on some plumbers in the high desert," said Matt. "In ten years everything between Victorville and Vegas will be paved."

"That's what we call the circle of life. As long as they're

building houses, we make money." Larry, shielding his eyes from the morning glare, looked out the window toward the parking lot. "Don't take this the wrong way, but your car is a piece of shit."

"It runs."

"Where was it made, Pyongyang?"

"It was my mom's car."

"Oh, right," said Larry, squinting briefly with concern. "Jack mentioned all that. Sorry to hear."

"Thanks."

Matt hated knowing that Jack was talking about him like some helpless and whimpering animal. But he also knew that it was his fault. For a year, around the office, he had cultivated such a persona. The polite mumbling, the wry but troubled smile, the faraway look in his eye—these devices, once real, were now more of a routine, a play for sympathy, allowing him to coast through his job. Matt pushed around the gravy on his chicken-fried steak.

"Listen," said Larry. "When I started in outside sales, Pete Dominic gave me some advice."

"Pete Dominic?"

"Yeah, Pete Dominic. Before his stroke, Pete was *the guy* at Mulhern Sales. Booster systems, vertical turbines, Pete killed it, top to bottom. He was one of the biggest assholes I ever met, but back then he was the only guy in L.A. who'd give me a chance to do outside sales. Before him, nobody would let me off the order desk. The other bosses I had liked me fine, but they didn't want my black ass walking through the door. Pete thought I could make him money, and I did. When he brought me on he said that if I wanted to make it selling industrial hydronics the first thing I should do is get a loan and buy the most expensive car possible. That way I'd have no choice but to bust my ass trying to pay for it."

Matt was pretty sure this was the worst advice anyone had ever given him, but he nodded and said, "Makes sense."

"I bought a Coup de Ville."

"Nice."

"It got repossessed after Mulhern went under, but that's a whole other story. That shit had nothing to do with me."

"I just want something that gets good mileage."

"Yeah, but you need style."

Matt felt slighted. He considered himself an industry fashion plate, if only because he refused to wear poofy pleats and knit golf shirts. One of his new customers, Ron Ciavacco, of Five Star Pipe and Supply in Baldwin Park, still wore Sansabelt pants.

"I can't afford a fancy car," Matt said.

"What else you spending your money on?"

"I'm saving for a trip to Europe."

"What's so great about Europe?"

"I don't know. Museums, cathedrals."

Larry laughed. "My first wife wanted us to go to Europe, but then she ran off with a Dominican."

"A priest?"

"A shortstop. Some single-A nobody making a hundred bucks a week." Larry put a cigarette in his mouth but didn't light it. "Are you going to finish that?"

Matt handed over what was left of his chicken-fried steak.

"Jack showed me your numbers," said Larry. "You're not exactly setting the world on fire."

"It's been rough."

"Jack thinks you're a lazy prima donna."

"I try not to be, but it goes against my instincts," said Matt, sounding waggish to cover the absolute truth of the statement.

"I don't tolerate laziness," said Larry. "It's a form of treason."

He began ripping open sugar packs and dumping them three at a time into his coffee.

"I have no sales experience and Jack doesn't believe in training."

"Baptism by fire," said Larry.

"It's been over a year and I still have no idea what I'm doing."

"Your job is to go out there every day and get your face kicked in. It's the only path to enlightenment."

"But I don't know what I'm selling," said Matt. "Once my contractors start talking spec I'm totally lost. They think I'm an idiot."

It was a relief for Matt to suddenly admit these things. Among his friends he was regarded as a talker and wiseass. But for the past year he had felt perpetually tongue-tied and back on his heels. He hated to ask people for anything, but that was the essence of sales. Whenever Jack or his dad asked him how he was doing out there, he would say he was doing fine. They wanted him to do well, but this was a business and they were losing patience.

Larry looked sympathetic. Finishing his coffee, he said, "I've known your old man a long time. He's a good salesman, but Christ, he's been doing it for thirty years. You get good after a while. Nobody's born with *a priori* knowledge of plumbing fixtures, or anything else. That's been proven by philosophy."

"We rep twenty-five lines. It's a lot to learn."

"So? You seem like a smart guy. Jack said you went to school."

"I never finished. I've been bartending and coaching soccer."

"Soccer?"

Larry said "soccer" with a vague distaste that Matt was used to. American men of a certain generation still associated the sport with communism and homosexuality.

"A JV team," said Matt.

The waitress brought the check and Larry grabbed it.

"I'll buy lunch," said Matt.

"Lunch is taken care of." Larry smiled. "We're going to the luau."

"It's an actual luau?"

"Yeah. They got beer, roast pig, everything. You're lucky I got you in there. These luaus are invite-only."

"Who's doing all this?"

"Lamrock."

For a moment the name lingered in the air, like someone had a struck a bell. Matt had heard of Lamrock. Plumbers throughout Los Angeles spoke his name in reverent whispers, though Matt could never quite figure out who he was or what he did. He asked his dad once, and Marty Costello said, "Lamrock's Lamrock. He's just somebody who knows everybody." During his first week at Ajax, Matt was standing on the loading dock with Jack, going over an order Matt had screwed up, when Linda, one of the inside sales girls, came running toward them. This was when she could still run—a month later, on her way home from work, she got caught in a drive-by on Redondo Beach Boulevard. Now there was a bullet in her spine and she was in a wheelchair. "Lamrock's on the line," she said, breathless. Jack, who usually kept no fewer than three people on hold at any given time, immediately ran back to the office.

"So who is Lamrock?" asked Matt.

"He's my guy in Boyle Heights."

"Is he a contractor or a wholesaler?"

"He's kind of both, and more too," said Larry, throwing a fifty on the table. "Lamrock's got his hand in a lot of pots."

Going west on PCH, they stopped at a liquor store. Matt waited in the car, listening to Jim Rome take a call from Terrence in Sierra Madre. Rome was an old SoCal, and before he got into radio he did time as an outside salesman. For some reason this gave Matt a strange sense of hope.

Larry came out wearing a new pair of wraparound sunglasses that made him look like an android assassin from the future. He bopped his head to unheard music and carried an armful of chips and Hostess cakes.

"Ho Ho?" he offered, getting back in the car.

"I'm stuffed."

"Do I look cool in these?" asked Larry, with a big a smile. The tag was still dangling in front of his nose.

Matt nodded.

"I bought us some Scratchers."

They both lost. Larry blew the silver scratchings across the dashboard.

"Sometimes I think I'll never win the lottery," he complained. "It's always some little Mexican guy from Guatemala with a million kids."

Matt, who was only eighteen units shy of his degree in history, winced slightly at this.

"You know what I mean," said Larry, sensing his disapproval. "Lord knows I'm cheering for those fucking people."

Matt's Nextel chirped. It was Jack.

"Is Larry still shitfaced?" he asked.

"He's right here."

"Good, I hope he's helping you out. Tell him if he doesn't write some business today, I'm going to drop Brentford and start repping Kenner."

Larry grabbed the phone out of Matt's hand.

"If you had the balls to bring in more inventory, your supply houses wouldn't complain so much about late shipments."

"My balls aren't the problem," said Jack.

Taking back the phone, Matt said, "We're on our way to Eagle Pipe. Hopefully, we'll get an order out of Armando."

"Hope is for pussies. Just get the order."

Jack chirped off. As Matt turned Jim Rome back on, Larry opened one of his bags.

"Cheeto?"

In his faded Chivas jersey, with its red and white vertical stripes bulging across his massive belly, Armando looked like a walking fumigation tent. He stood behind the will call counter, holding a sprinkled donut in one hand and a ping-pong paddle in the other.

"I think I remember you," he said, squinting at Larry. He put down his paddle and shook Larry's hand.

"Didn't Chet what's-his-name used to manage this branch?" Larry asked.

"Chet died last year," said Armando, making the sign of the cross with his donut. "He had a stroke on the eleventh hole at El Dorado."

"Chet moved a lot of Brentford," said Larry. "Back when he was alive."

"So did I, before the recall."

"The ballcocks. Jesus, man. You know we're taking care of that shit. The best we can. Has Matt talked to you about the new Ultima?"

"I gave him the new catalogue," Matt said.

"A monkey can pass out catalogues," said Larry. "You go over it with him?"

"Yeah, he did, pretty much," said Armando, slapping Matt on the shoulder. "You guys want a drink?"

Like a lot of guys in the industry, Armando had worked his way up from the bottom. He started as a driver, moved into the warehouse, worked the will call counters, did purchasing, and eventually became a manager. He had a knack for remembering part numbers. All day long he'd sit behind the counter like a bard, singing to the lesser poets in back ("Compression stops, OR12s, half inch!"). More importantly, for Matt, he was a big soccer fan. Matt followed the Mexican league, so they always had something to talk about. It was so much easier than actually asking for an order.

Back in the warehouse the air smelled sour from the diesel exhaust of forklifts. A few guys were eating chorizo-and-egg burritos at a cheap plastic table that had as its centerpiece a gleaming metropolis of half-empty Tapatío bottles. Armando opened a fridge and grabbed two Cokes.

"Is that the last *cerveza*, amigo?" asked Larry, peering inside.

"Take it," said Armando. "I got more in back."

"I told Armando we would get him the new Ultima to display up front."

"We can do that," said Larry, trying to twist off the cap. "We can definitely do that."

"I want it free," said Armando. "Mike from Southwestern hooked me up with a free Kenner model."

Mike Melendez, a snake, worked at Southwestern Sales, a rival rep company from Gardena. He had a knack for showing up at wholesalers a few minutes before Matt arrived, offering deals on Kenner products and reminding purchasing agents about the nightmare that was the Brentford ballcock recall.

"I don't know if we can do *that*," said Larry, bending forward to get better leverage on the cap.

"Those aren't twist-offs, man," said Armando.

"I've got an opener," offered Matt, but it was too late.

Larry had ripped off the cap, along with a layer of skin on his right palm. Blood dripped down his hand as he took the first sip. "Just bring it in on consignment."

The word "consignment" made Matt think of the circles of hell; he still only had a vague idea what it meant in the commercial sense.

"That works for me," said Armando, shrugging. "Let me write it up."

This happened now and then, a sale. It always made Matt more giddy than he expected, and in those moments he understood why some men kept grinding away year after year.

Later, over a game of ping-pong, they talked about Brentford's new urinals and Armando suggested they chase down a mechanical contractor he knew in Carson who was bidding a job for L.A. Unified.

"We could see him before we hit the luau," suggested Larry, pressing a wad of toilet paper into his palm.

Armando interrupted his serve. "Lamrock's?"

"Are you going?" asked Larry.

"Oh, yeah," said Armando, firing a wicked ball past Matt. "Anybody who's got anything to do with anything will be there."

"Who's Lamrock?" asked Matt.

"Do you have a Hawaiian shirt?" Armando asked Matt.

"No."

Armando looked ominously at Larry.

"What happens if I don't have a Hawaiian shirt?" asked Matt, beginning to panic. "Who's Lamrock?"

They drove north on Cherry Avenue, past the gates of All Souls Cemetery. For the past year, whenever he called on customers in Long Beach, Matt would swing by All Souls to look at his mother's tombstone. He'd stand there for a while, trying to remember everything about her, every moment they ever shared, but strangely he couldn't remember very much. His mind, for the most part, was a searing blank. Now and then he'd remember something small and meaningless from her last year, things he saw when he drove her to doctor appointments or watched television with her in the afternoon. He could see the shadows of the parking garage at St. Joseph Hospital, but he couldn't see her. This felt like a curse and he worried that he had failed her in some way. He hated himself for not finishing school, for not establishing his place in the world. If he ever made anything of himself, she would never see it.

When he moved home it felt like a relief because he had a purpose; each day he knew exactly what he had to do, and nobody expected anything more from him. They watched all the home makeover shows together. His sisters also moved back home. Everybody was together. When his dad and sisters got back from work and school, relieving him of his duties, Matt would go play pickup soccer games at an abandoned junior high, using what Spanish he knew to scream for the ball. It was the same field he played on as a kid and sometimes he expected to look up and see his mom in her lawn chair, sucking on a menthol and cursing the referee. For years she labored under the delusion that Matt got fouled every time he touched the ball. Her shrill and partisan commentary from the sidelines had once embarrassed Matt, but now, as an adult, playing with strangers at twilight on a field full of weeds and gopher holes, he wanted to hear some distant echo of her voice, fighting for him and believing in his cause, whatever the fuck that was.

A few weeks earlier, while walking through the cemetery, Matt had seen his dad in the distance, already at the tombstone, standing above it, in his brown Members Only jacket, with his arms folded and his frizzy comb-over flapping in the wind. It was two o'clock, that dreaded time of day when outside salesmen suddenly find themselves alone after a busy morning. Matt suspected that every outside salesmen looked for ways to escape this bright and desolate hour. Pubs, libraries, the beach—Matt had all his sanctuaries mapped out. Twenty minutes to himself, outside of his car, that's all he wanted. The cemetery was a frequent stop. He hid behind a tree so his father couldn't see him.

What this man did when he left the house every morning had once been a mystery, but now Matt knew. Apparently Marty Costello had busted his ass for three decades, covering every godforsaken territory in SoCal and establishing a reputation as a resourceful and good-humored sales rep. Sometimes business was good, sometimes it wasn't. The boom-and-bust life of a salesman meant that the house in Anaheim had been mortgaged multiple times, and it was only a matter of time, Matt knew, before the bank took it back entirely. Instead of land, his dad had left him the only thing he truly owned: the freeways.

Matt used to wonder what his dad thought about as he drove the freeways all day, every day, and it made him sad to think that this man, who never complained about anything, might have dreamed about doing something else with his life besides selling toilets. But Matt realized now, with envy, that his father had moved beyond dreams. He belonged to this world, day after day. In a dusty waterworks supply on the outskirts of Barstow, which was on the outskirts of nowhere, Matt had met Woody Blake, another plumbing lifer whose body, like a Joshua tree, had been hunched and twisted over the years by the high desert wind. Holding a pit bull on a leash, Woody greeted Matt in his trailer office and said, "Costello? Any relation to Marty?"

"He's my dad."

"I've known Marty for years. He's a good guy."

That day in the cemetery Matt knew if he kept walking he and his dad would see each other, a pair of truants, and they would laugh. It was what the Costellos did best when they were together and it had saved them from almost everything. But Matt didn't want to share a laugh. He wanted to be alone with her, just for a few minutes, before getting back on the freeway.

In a trance, Matt hit his turn signal for the cemetery, but then saw Larry wiping orange Cheeto dust all over his khakis and remembered where he was. Larry reached back for his briefcase, put it in his lap, and popped it open. Matt glanced over and saw that it was empty except for two neatly folded Hawaiian shirts.

"Better safe than sorry," he said.

"Why would we be sorry?"

"You'd be sorry, not me. You're just lucky I brought an extra."

"Why is it so important I wear a Hawaiian shirt?"

Larry looked at him like he was crazy. "Because it's a fucking luau, son."

Matt turned onto Del Amo and for a few intersections they drove in silence. As they crossed the L.A. River, Larry's cell phone rang.

"Yeah, babe . . . The box is in the garage, next to my roller skates . . . Okay, 'bye." Larry flipped his phone shut and rolled his eyes at Matt. "Juanita, my fiancée. She's looking for the good silverware."

"Congratulations."

"For what?"

"Getting engaged."

"She'll be number four. She was also number two."

Matt was quiet for a moment, trying to do the math.

"She's got MS," said Larry. "She needs someone around to listen to her bitch."

Matt turned briefly to Larry, who stared straight ahead. They turned off into an industrial park and found the address. Fred Tuiolosega, the proprietor of Gateway Plumbing, greeted them wearing shorts and a Hawaiian shirt. Behind him two enormous young men with shaved heads were working the phones.

"The luau is already out of control," he told them. "We just stayed long enough to say hi to Lamrock."

Fred walked barefoot through a tiny office adorned with high school football trophies and BYU pennants. A big, thick man, with arms like fresh-cut logs, he perched on a stool as

Larry awkwardly reached out his left hand for a shake. He un-zipped his fanny pack and handed Fred his card. When Matt reached in his pocket to do the same, he found it empty. He turned red, knowing how bush league it would look running out to his car to grab more cards from the trunk.

Larry asked about the L.A. Unified job. Fred said the spec was for Kenner, but he'd switch to Brentford if their ballcock thing was fixed. He gave Larry the spec sheets, and Larry gave them to Matt to give them to Jack to give them to Linda, in the Ajax office, to run a price quote and send it to Armando, who would send it back to Fred. It was a strange and mystifying calculus. The factory sold to the rep, the rep to the whole-saler, the wholesaler to the contractor, but sometimes the rep skipped a step and talked directly to the contractor, telling him which wholesaler to buy from, so the wholesaler would have no choice but to buy a particular line from the rep. Matt was lost somewhere in the middle.

"*Muy bien*," said Larry, once everything was sorted. "How's everything else going?"

"Business is good right now," said Fred. He waved his arm around the office. "The Lord's really blessed us."

"I know how that goes," said Larry. "As long as we're talk-ing that . . ." Larry folded his arms. "The other day I caught my stepson on the computer looking at things he shouldn't be looking at. Some really nasty stuff. Nasty, *nasty* stuff."

Fred, looking genuinely aggrieved, shook his head.

"Six or seven dudes with their business out," said Larry, "and there's one chick in the middle, just *going* for it."

The giant Tuiolosega boys looked up from their phones.

"I've got the new Brentford catalogue if you want it," said Matt.

"So we had a talk," Larry continued, "and the next day, all on his own, he went down to our church and told the pastor he wanted to rededicate himself to Christ."

"Good for him," said Fred. "It's easy for kids to get screwed up these days."

As a gesture of dismissal, Fred handed Larry and Matt his card.

Larry reached into his fanny pack and took out a colorful bundle of cards and loose scraps of paper. "Let me upload you into the system here," he said, placing Fred's card on top.

"I'm out of cards," mumbled Matt. "I'll go grab one."

"Don't worry about it," said Fred, walking them out.

Back in the car, Larry took a deep breath. "I think I fucked that up."

"It's okay," said Matt. "I'll check in with them later this week."

"Sometimes the mouth moves faster than the brain," said Larry. "But at least I was talking. You can't just stand there like that. You gotta open your damn mouth."

They got on the 710 north, a blind and savage freeway. The lanes were choked with freight trucks coming up from the harbor. Matt's Kia was dwarfed on all sides by smoke-belching eighteen-wheelers. Shadows crept over him and he lost sight of the sky. The farther he got from the coast, the more claustrophobic he felt. Driving inland was like being lowered into a pit.

Larry, rummaging through the glove compartment for a tissue, found a battered copy of Catch-22. It was one of the few books Matt had saved from high school and he had picked it up recently.

"I never read this," Larry said, flipping the pages. "Is it good?"

"It's fucking great!" Matt heard his voice go up an octave; he coughed and tried to take it down a notch. "My dad read it while he was in Vietnam. Can you believe that?"

"I used to read a ton on the road. All that legal thriller crap."

"I've read a bunch of Grishams," said Matt.

"What's your favorite?"

"I don't know," said Matt, trying to remember which one was which.

"*A Time to Kill* is his best book," said Larry, "and can I tell you why in two words: Matthew-fucking-what's-his-name. He's a great actor when he wants to be." Larry examined his bloody hand. "Did you read *The Bridges of Madison County*?"

"Sort of." Matt thought of all the crappy books on tape his mom listened to during her chemo sessions and he thought of all the Sandra Bullock romantic comedies they watched together at home in the afternoons. He'd squirm during the melodramatic parts. She often wondered aloud how she and her husband, with twelve credits of junior college between them, had managed to raise children who were such snobs. But now, whenever he saw one of those terrible movies on cable, he'd watch it, waiting for the melodramatic parts where she used to choke up. It was a sick way to make himself cry.

"I think Meryl Streep shows her tits in that," said Larry, lighting a cigarette. "But for my money, *Crimson Tide* is the best movie ever made."

"I'd probably disagree with you there," said Matt.

"David Spade hasn't been in anything good in a while," continued Larry, connecting a mysterious series of dots. "Not since *Three Amigos*."

"He's not in that," said Matt, with a sudden note of authority in his voice.

"Who am I thinking of?"

"I don't know."

"David Spade. He was on *Just Kill Me*, right?"

"*Just Shoot Me*. Right."

"He was also in the other thing. With Pauly Shore and the other guy."

"I'm not sure what you're talking about."

"What movie am I thinking of?"

"I don't know."

"Was it *Valley Dude*?"

"I don't think so."

"He wasn't in *Valley Dude*?"

"I don't think that's an actual movie."

"I think I'm thinking of what's-his-name. The other guy."

These were the kind of looping and erroneous cultural discussions Matt tended to have with his mom. He had a sudden urge to write it all down, every pointless word.

They were passing over the lost industrial cities of Bell, Cudahy, and Vernon, a flatulent corridor of derelict foundries and abandoned railroad spurs. In the distance, through the bright, murky haze, the downtown buildings looked like they were sitting in a jar of formaldehyde.

"I miss the road," Larry said. "I miss the action."

"The driving gets to me," admitted Matt.

"Yeah, but it's better than being holed up in some office."

They made a brief stop in City of Commerce to see Ron Ciavacco at Five Star, but his sister, Valerie, who did all the purchasing, explained that Ron was at a doctor's appointment. He hadn't been feeling well. Without looking up from the invoice pile she was sorting, she coughed and said, "His heart."

Matt drove east on Washington and then took Soto north toward Boyle Heights. After spending the morning on the freeway, circling through lifeless industrial zones, it was nice to see people on the street, waiting at bus stops, pushing strollers, crowding around the *frutas frescas* men. They passed the old Sears distribution center, a giant art deco relic. Larry had him turn left and they came to an empty road that ran alongside the stark, geometric banks of the Los Angeles River. The sloping concrete walls absorbed the sunlight and pulsed with an alien phosphorescent whiteness. Matt turned away from the hypnotic glare and saw a dead rooster in the middle of the street.

"Chupacabras," said Larry.

They passed a series of vandalized warehouses and came finally to a long cinder-block fence crowned with barbed wire. A dozen or so cars were parked on the street. They got out and Larry removed the Hawaiian shirts from his briefcase.

"Do you want hula girls or palm trees?"

"Hula girls."

"Take the palm trees. The hula girls is kind of tacky."

Farther down, a couple plumbers wearing bandannas, cut-off Dickies, and bright red Hawaiian shirts walked through the gate, each with a twelve-pack under his arm. The air was filled with acrid smoke.

Going through the gates, they passed a dark, lanky bald man with a thick mustache. He was leaning heavily against a stack of pallets, trying without success to pour a bottle of Bacardi into a can of Coke. He lifted his head and fixed his bloodshot eyes on Larry's shirt. "Brentford sucks!"

"What did you say?" said Larry.

"Your ballcocks are fucked, man!"

"Who the fuck are you?"

"That's Mike Melendez," said Matt. "He's the Kenner rep."

"Fuck Brentford!"

"I don't have to listen to this." Larry unzipped his fanny pack and took out a gun.

"Jesus Christ," said Matt.

"Don't worry," Larry told him. "It's loaded."

Matt couldn't take his eyes off the gun. He felt, instinctively, that if he turned away, a bullet would rip open the back of his skull and his body would be dumped in the river. Mike, for his part, was not impressed. He made a dismissive propeller sound with his lips and took a swig of his Bacardi and Coke. "Whatever," he said, shuffling away.

"Like Kenner's never had a recall," said Larry, looking bewildered and disappointed as he returned the gun to his fanny pack. "Lamrock is definitely gonna hear about this."

"Are you fucking nuts?" said Matt.

"Calm down, everything's fine," said Larry. "Lamrock loves guns."

"*Who?* Who the fuck is Lamrock?"

"Come on. I'll introduce you."

Matt's head dropped. He rubbed his eyes. "You said there's beer?"

"Yeah, there's beer."

They went through the gates into a large pipe yard. Plumbers were milling around, eating off paper plates, talking on their Nextels. They passed through the warehouse, where workers buzzed around, racing each other on pallet jacks, and exited down the open steps of the loading dock. A big blond woman in a yellow muumuu called them over.

"I figured you'd show," she greeted Larry, kissing him on the cheek. She had a bag full of plastic leis and ceremoniously placed one over each of their heads.

"Good to see you, Wanda," said Larry. He introduced Matt and tugged on his shirt. "Look at this kid, all breezed out."

"That's a nice one," she said.

"What happens if you don't wear a shirt?"

"You don't want to know," she said.

"I'd really like to know."

She swept her flabby arm across the scene of the luau. He saw a cracked and weedy slab of concrete sloping down to the railroad tracks, with dramatic views of the septic river and the cluster of buildings downtown. The yard was strewn with old toilets and mangled pipe. Plumbers and wholesalers stood in a buffet line, where mounds of kalua pork were piled on their plate. A bunch of guys, including Armando, were standing around lighting fireworks. Woody Blake, the waterworks man from Barstow, was showing off his pit bull.

"If you don't have a shirt," she said, "you can't be in the raffle."

Matt laughed. He wanted a beer.

"Grand prize is dinner for two at Olive Garden," she said.

"I'll never win that fucking raffle," said Larry, taking his ticket.

They grabbed Coronas out of an old bathtub filled with ice and made their way to the buffet line, where Matt ran into Ron Ciavacco.

"Don't tell Valerie I'm here," he pleaded, adjusting his elastic pants. "She thinks I'm at the doctor."

"Give us an order," said Larry, "and we won't say a word."

"That's extortion."

"It's business."

"This your first luau?" Ron asked Matt.

"Yeah. Larry pulled a gun on Mike Melendez."

"I heard."

"Come on," Larry said. "Let's find Lamrock."

They walked to the far end of the pipe yard, which looked like an abandoned flea market. Matt saw televisions and VCRs, washers and dryers, coffee tables, empty jewelry counters, bicycles, pianos, surfboards, and a crumbling pyramid of tires. They found him passed out in an empty Jacuzzi shell. Lamrock was a chubby little man with with a gray crew cut. He wore red swim trucks with black socks and sandals. There was a shotgun next to his head and he had a small handgun holstered on his ankle.

"So what is he?" Matt asked. "A wholesaler?"

"More of a distributor," said Ron, tentatively. "But a contractor too, I guess. On the general side of things."

"I'll tell you what he is," said Larry, holding his beer up in salute. "He's a goddamn angel."

After lunch, Larry offered to let Matt fire off a few rounds into the empty river. "No way," said Matt. "I'm scared of guns."

Lamrock eventually rose from his slumber and Larry introduced him to Matt. Lamrock raised his beer and said, "Here's to ya." Then he stumbled away. Later Matt saw him at the far end of the lot, aiming his shotgun at the ironwork of a distant railroad trestle. A crowd of drunk plumbers cheered him on.

— 190 —

Matt finally wandered away from the crowd and sat down on a rusty toilet.

It was two o'clock, that bright and desolate hour. Matt couldn't believe where he was. A year ago, when people stopped by to see his mom, they would often ask him, once they had left her room, what he was going to do "after." It seemed like an irrelevant question, and he never had an answer. He would just walk them to the front door and return to her room. The walls were covered with family photos, a crucifix, and a framed map of Ireland. In the afternoons he opened the curtains and the glass slider, letting in the breeze and giving his mom a view of the pool. Twenty years ago, during one of the booms, the Costellos had put in the pool. It was their greatest triumph as a family. They probably should've saved the money to get them through the next bust, but Ellen Costello wanted her kids to have a pool. She gave her children everything she had and more, heedless of cost, and Matt knew that he owed much of his happiness to his parents' willingness to live beyond their means.

A million things about his mom should've made Matt nostalgic, but for some reason the time he longed for most was the last couple months of her life. They rarely spoke about anything important, but they had never been closer. Her suffering was beyond words and Matt knew that the frail, bed-bound woman in front of him was the toughest person he would ever meet. He wanted to be with her again, in hell, shifting her pillows, changing her TPN bags, rinsing her vomit bowls. Those afternoons destroyed him and would continue to destroy him every day of his life. For this he was thankful. He needed to be destroyed.

Matt liked to think that the last thing his mom saw, before she died, was the tranquil surface of the pool.

"There you are," he heard Larry saying. Matt looked up and saw him silhouetted against the bright sky. Larry handed him a beer. "We're celebrating."

"Why?"

"Because you're quitting."

"I am?"

Larry took a sip of beer and looked out across the river. "Just be glad you got to see the luau."

"Thanks for bringing me."

"You're not a salesman."

"I wish I was."

"Go do something else," said Larry, and there was mercy in his voice. "Don't waste our time down here."

Part II: Costello

Costello sees a lizard at the bottom of the pool. The sucker is dead, dead. Full fathom five, as they say. This lizard situation, on a Saturday, presents a major hassle. Costello stands barefoot on the diving board, bouncing a little, with an unlit Tareyton between his lips. Saturday, an extra layer of brightness, Saturday brightness, like God opening a window in the sky.

The backyard needs some work. Weeds flaming up from cracks in the concrete, all the flower pots empty, the patio cover rotten with termites. Costello pops a net onto the aluminum pole and stands at the edge of the deep end. His wife wanted the deep end extra deep, so the kids could dive. The water is green, the lizard caught in silhouette, his tail wedged underneath the filter cover. Costello scoops up a flotilla of dead june bugs, dumps them in the planter, and then goes deeper, making a play for the lizard.

Next door, Jesse Rocha starts up his hedge trimmer. He's the same age as Costello, but semiretired. By some dull, suburban coincidence Rocha, like Costello, is also a plumbing lifer, but on the skilled side of things, repairs and remodels, three trucks and a shop. Last year, finessing his way out of a worker's comp lawsuit, he changed the company name from Rocha Plumbing to Advanced Plumbing Specialists. "This is the great state of California," he said. "Sunshine and litigation."

Rocha pokes his bald head over the brown cinder-block wall, the same crumbling wall that squares off every yard in this section of Anaheim. He turns off the trimmer.

"Hey, Marty," he says. "I saw that thing in the *Pipeline*. Congratulations."

It came yesterday, the new issue of the *Pipeline*, quarterly organ of the West Coast Plumbing Association. Twelve pages, two staples. Martin Costello, a nominee for sales rep of the year.

"I'm working on my acceptance speech," Costello says.

Rocha laughs. He and Connie are nice enough, always helpful. A common-law thing, no kids. Hedging their bets for twenty years.

"You should hire our pool guy," Rocha says.

"I don't mind doing it."

"Your water looks a little green."

"I'll blow it up with chemicals," Costello says. "Nagasaki the shit out of it." Points to the deep end. "There's a lizard down there. At the bottom."

"I thought lizards could swim."

"I'm not sure."

"Crocodiles can swim," Rocha says. "A crocodile is just a big lizard."

"I know salamanders can swim."

"That's true."

"They're amphibious," Costello says.

"My grandma used to keep axolotls." Rocha spells the word for him. "Mexican salamanders," he explains. "Milky white, with golden eyes. They'd freak you out."

"Golden eyes? Holy shit."

Nods, silence. A meeting of the minds. Two medieval doctors.

"You're not swimming, are you?" Rocha asks. "The water's a little green."

"I'm just gonna float around on the raft."

The trimmer cracks on, the noise a million tiny cracks in the afternoon.

Costello is shirtless, his belly soft and pink. Still wearing his old Dodgers cap. He hasn't combed his hair on a Saturday in thirty years, not since before the kids were born. He flips the cap around so he can see what he's doing. The long pole rests against his shoulder; he pushes it under the lizard, but the poor sucker won't budge. Costello gives up.

His sacraments wait for him by the shallow-end steps. Sports page, crossword puzzle, felt-tip pen, the Tareytons, three left, and a Zippo flashing in the sun. And the new issue of the *Pipeline*. A bit of vanity. He climbs carefully onto the plastic raft and pushes off the side, off the tile that she chose, orange and purple, a floral mosaic, Spanish.

A nice day, warm and clear. What they call an azure sky. On the wooden telephone pole in the corner of the yard a single crow keeps vigil. The telephone wires run parallel to everything. The sky divided by clean horizontal lines: the roof, the wall, the wires. This is what he paid for. Peaceful ranch house living. Sea-green stucco and a sliding glass door.

Three mortgages, babe, each one more magnificent than the last.

Costello is looking at himself. Page three of the *Pipeline*, a feature article about the company he works for, Ajax Plumbing Sales, of Compton. Special notices to Jack Isahakian, the owner, who is nominated for manager of the year, and to him, Martin Costello, the top outside guy. The supreme council of elders will announce the awards this Friday, after the annual

WCPA Best Ball Extravaganza. Every contractor, rep, and wholesaler in SoCal descending on whatever shitball municipal golf course the council has managed to rent out. The hackfest of all hackfests.

Costello is pictured merrily athwart a brand-new Ultima 900, which he specified onto every track house built last year in the high desert by Progressive Plumbing, Inc. (formerly Lamrock & Hoon LLC). The defective ballcocks on the Ultimas are still causing problems—a nightmare sorting the warranty situation with the factory—but the article doesn't mention that. A nice fluff piece. Jack, in his humility, made the photographer put the entire Ajax crew in the picture, inside sales, outside sales, warehouse crew, everybody hanging off forklifts and pallets in the sunny pipe yard. Everybody squinting, faces bright. Linda—pronounced *Leenda*—in her wheelchair, waving to the camera. Next to the forklift, Costello's son, Matt, the picture taken a couple weeks before he gave up plumbing to finish his degree, God bless. The article extols Ajax's transformation after the brutalities of the last housing crash, the bust years, 1989–95, the trifecta mortgage years. Jack Isahakian, quoted at length: "We got fat on new construction like everybody else, but when reality set in we had to change things, think smaller, master the nickle and dime stuff with our wholesalers." All the news that's fit to print.

Rocha finishes whacking his bottlebrush plant, turns the trimmer off. Costello, drifting in the deep end, sees a cloud of red needles floating over the wall.

"We're turning on the barbecue tonight," says Rocha. "Feel free to come by."

A year of warm regards and kind invitations. A year of telling lies to avoid them.

"I'm meeting the kids for dinner," says Costello. "Thanks, though."

Rocha salutes and leaves the wall. A moment later the sound of his diving board, then a splash of impressive magnitude. Jesse Rocha, a virtuoso of the cannonball.

Costello lights up. Tareyton, the taste we're fighting for. No more sneaking them. Killing himself out in the open, under a blue sky.

Costello drifts for a few minutes, blowing smoke rings, idly snapping the Zippo. Nice and quiet. A dragonfly hovers over the water, touching down smooth and fast, then gone, zigzagging up and over the wall, a dust-off.

The telephone pole in the corner of the yard, like the mainmast of a ship. Galleons and caravels. Sailors in the crosstrees on lookout. Magellan and his crew, drifting on the equator, praying for wind.

Costello starts the crossword, but can't concentrate. An uneasy feeling clutches his stomach. The lizard directly below, full fathom five. He pushes off toward the shallow end and disembarks, his feet slipping into the slimy water.

Evening comes. The house is dark. Costello drives his Pontiac Grand Am one block, parks in a cul-de-sac, and walks back to the house, slipping in through the side gate. Smoke and mirrors, to make the Rochas think he's out with the kids. The Rochas always knock a second time, asking again if he wants to come over.

Later, in his recliner, in the dark, with the curtains drawn and the air-conditioning blasting, he turns on the game. The voice of Vin Scully, soothing and omniscient, the God voice of SoCal. Costello gets nervous during games. He paces the green shag in the family room, looking for distractions. The upper shelves of the wall unit are full of pictures, Katie and Matt and Megan, as kids, in various stages of toothlessness and rec league glory. Then the encyclopedias, Funk & Wagnalls, A through Z, one a month at Safeway for two years. Costello wants to look up axolotls, but "A" is missing. There's a copy of *Moby-Dick*. Some other random books of nautical lore. Krakens, mermaids, the fata morgana. Costello finds the book of explorers, turns to his favorite passage. Magellan's crew, lost in the doldrums of the Pacific, slowly starving to death. Costello, laughing, reads his favorite quote: ". . . and when they ran out of rats, they chewed the bark off the mainmast."

In the kitchen, by the light of the refrigerator, Costello takes out a giant bag of hot dogs. Then a giant tub of mustard, then a giant tub of mayonnaise. Smart & Final, apocalypse shopping. He puts dogs on a paper plate, shoves them in the microwave. Waiting, he sets up four buns, slapping on mustard and mayonnaise. He takes a fifth bun, balls it up, dips it in the mayonnaise, swallows it whole. The dogs pop and hiss. He pours Pepsi from a two-liter bottle into a clean glass just out of the dishwasher. A bit of decorum. The television illuminates the family room, waves of blue, aquarium light. Costello, leaning forward in his recliner, a dish towel over his knees, eyes focused on the game, mayonnaise punctuating both sides of his mouth—this is how he eats. The kids are trying to get him out more. It's been over a year, they say, you need to get out there, you need to do something, go somewhere. Go where? We've got the pool.

In the bottom of the ninth a pinch hitter stares innocently at strike three. Costello throws his cap at the television, stomps down the dark hall. For a while he plays hearts on the

computer, sipping his Pepsi, trying to calm down. His ani-
mated opponents are a bear, an alien, and some kind of go-go
dancer. At ten o'clock, hearing the Disneyland fireworks, he
can't help himself. He goes out through the garage, scales the
side gate onto the roof, and walks barefoot across the asphalt
shingles. An old summer ritual, watching fireworks on the roof,
his pool and Rocha's sparkling in the darkness, the kids tossing
their Popsicle sticks down the chimney. He lights up, snaps
the Zippo. Down below he sees Rocha and Connie, holding
beers, watching the sky. They hear something, start looking
around. Connie, ten years younger than Rocha, firm as all hell,
what they call a biker babe. *Thou shalt not covet.* Soon they'll
notice the man lurking above them. They will ask legitimate
questions and listen generously to his implausible answers.
This is bad form, weird and selfish behavior, blowing them off
to watch the game alone. They are nice enough people.

Costello, on tiptoe, moves toward the chimney, the only
hiding place, but he trips on one of the support wires that hold
up the old TV aerial. He rolls down the slant, but the chimney
catches him before he can plunge into the dead rosebushes.
Cursing silently to himself, he hears Rocha.

"Marty? Is that you?"

"Marty, are you okay?" Connie calls in her raspy voice.

Costello crouches behind the chimney. A night ambush.
The sky cracking, turning colors. Surrender.

"Yeah," he says, standing up, faking laughter. "I tripped."

"Don't fall off the roof, man," Rocha says.

"Look," Costello says, pointing in the general direction of
the Matterhorn. "Here comes the grand finale."

Greens and blues and reds, whirling and cracking. Connie
claps when it's over.

"I'll see you Friday, Marty," Rocha says, squeezing Connie's ass.

"You will?"

"The WCPA tourney," Rocha reminds him.

"Right," Costello says. "Ajax is sponsoring a hole. Stop by if you want."

An hour later, with his bloody foot wrapped in toilet paper, he watches the local news, waiting for sports and weather.

Sunday, Costello arrives late to evening mass, sits in the back, falls asleep during the homily, then slips out right after Communion, still chewing the wafer as he hurries across the parking lot. Francine, the parish retard, accosts him. Forty going on ten. Not enough oxygen to the brain at birth. Acne, hairy upper lip, one of God's defectives. Lives in a halfway house down the street. She rides around on a beach cruiser, greeting people, keeping track of who goes to mass, spreading her tragic brand of glee. His wife was friends with Francine, or put up with her, at least, let her stop by the house, let her ramble on and on. For a while, afterward, Francine came by to visit Costello. He'd hold the door half closed, smile, feign sleep, illness, never letting her in. A responder to subtle hints Francine is not.

She rolls toward him on her bike.

"Hi, Marty!"

"Hey, there, Francine," Costello says, swallowing the consecrated host. "Shouldn't you be wearing a helmet?"

Keys, door, faster. A fucking zombie attack.

" 'Bye, Marty!"

•　•　•

On Monday morning Costello neatly arranges his hair cross-wise over his skull using a comb, a blow dryer, and an aerosol product called "The Dry Look." Pleated khakis, beige golf shirt with Ajax logo, brown Members Only jacket. Everything you own is brown, she said. He clicks the Nextel into his belt holster and leaves the house at six o'clock.

Anaheim is beautiful. Supremo freeway access in all directions. All that concrete crisscrossing in the air, north and south, east and west, a compass rose. He takes the 91, the Artesia Freeway, east toward the Ajax warehouse in Compton. The freeway all to himself. Dick Dale on cassette, black coffee from McDonald's, a trunk full of defective ballcocks. He checks the odometer: 237,000 and counting. He averages 50,000 miles per year, vast territories, circles of latitude, Inglewood to Barstow, sailing across SoCal, all day, every day. Thirty-five years, carry the one, that's a couple million miles. Circumnavigation. Begin where you end, end where you begin. Sailors crossing the equator, initiated into the ancient mysteries of the deep. Getting laid in the watery parts of the world. In Hong Kong, R&R, the house on the hill, his first and only piece before her. Fifty thousand miles per year. Let them bury Martin Costello on the freeway. Let them throw his body over the side of a transition loop, commending his soul to *Trafficus rex.*

He exits the 91, cruises down Avalon Boulevard, turns left into an industrial cul-de-sac. Pigeons and graffiti and concertina wire. Costello parks next to Jack Isahakian's Mercury Grand Marquis. Luis, the Lord of Will Call, walks out of the Ajax warehouse, on his way to get breakfast at the roach coach, which has entered the cul-de-sac, horn blaring. The sun is coming up.

An exchange of *que pasos*, and then Costello asks, "You ever see an axolotl?"

Luis, eyes still bloodshot after his festival weekend in Zacatecas, shakes his head.

"It's a Mexican salamander," Costello explains.

"I saw a gila monster," says Luis.

"I've seen pictures of those things," says Costello. "Ugly suckers."

"The thing about them," says Luis, "is they don't have . . . they can't ever . . ."

"They can't ever what?"

"The tail just gets bigger," says Luis. "It fills up. Their whole life."

"What, with shit?" Costello readies a Tareyton. "Are you telling me gila monsters don't have assholes?"

"It just fills up."

"That's not healthful. Shit is toxic."

Costello considers a burrito. It will destroy him, but what the hell. He and Luis load up on chorizo and enter the pipe yard. Sunlight playing through a pyramid of bell-ended sixteen-inch PVC. The warehouse is twenty thousand square feet. Smells sweetly of diesel exhaust. Costello walks up the ramp that Jack installed for Linda and enters the dark and empty office. He passes through the catalogue library and into Jack's wood-paneled war room. Jack is a giant eyebrow with a man attached. He's already on the phone with one of the factories. On his desk a double frame with pictures of his wife and kids.

Fluorescent light and the smell of a million burned coffees.

"Hold on," Jack says, and puts his hand over the mouth-piece. "Listen, comrade. I'm sending out an email. I'm outlaw-ing consignments. Anything we ship from here we expect to be paid for. That's my new business philosophy. I'm speaking, what do you call it? Ex cathedra? You guys have too many funky arrangements going, and I'm too stupid to keep track. If you want, do sixty-day billing and address the receivable with Linda, but after that point we expect to be paid. That's what I'm going to say in the email."

"Gila monsters don't have assholes," Costello says, sitting down.

"Can I call you back?" Jack hangs up the phone. "Is that true?"

"The tail just gets bigger. The shit stores up in there and that's why they're poisonous."

"That makes sense from an evolution standpoint."

"Good thing humans don't work like that," Costello says. "That would be a major blow to our industry."

"Beautiful." Jack sips from his Styrofoam cup. "Listen. You need to talk to somebody at Bromberg. We need to get this ballcock thing taken care of once and for all."

"It's taken care of," Costello says. "That's all I've been doing. Lamrock was merciful. He signed off on everything."

"I'm still getting calls from everybody at Bromberg."

"One defective part and the whole universe unravels."

"I'm tired of the calls. I can't deal with those fucking people."

"I'm going out there on Thursday," Costello says. "I'll take care of it."

"Great," Jack says. "How's everything else?"

"Have you ever seen an axolotl? It's a white lizard with golden eyes."

"No, but there's a bat in Paraguay that can fly through trees. It's got a powerful sonar. The sonar makes a hole in the tree and the thing flies right through."

"Things can't fly through other things," says Costello. "That's one of the laws of physics."

Jack shrugs, sips his coffee. This is the best part of the morning, bullshitting with Jack. Another lifer. Costello met him in 1972, when he was with Henderson Sales of Gardena, his first real gig. Started three weeks after his discharge. In the interview all they really wanted to know was if he played softball. They needed a shortstop. Destiny. Two years on the order desk, then inside sales, enjoying the air-conditioning. Then outside sales, flying around the country, a briefcase man, calling on big accounts in Kalamazoo, Adamsville, Port Arthur, and other cosmopolitan places. Phoning her every night from those ratty motel rooms. They once sent him to New York, his first and only time. He had visions of marble and light, a weekend full of banter, highballs, limousines, just like in the movies. But he was only there for twelve hours, taking a cab from JFK directly to a national distro center in Bedford-Stuyvesant. He did his presentation for all the managers and purchasing agents, and on the way out he met a valves rep coming through the door, Jack Isahakian, of the Glendale Isahakians, also on the East Coast for one day. An hour later, in the rain, they shared a cab back to JFK, neither of them so much as glimpsing the Manhattan skyline. It always turns out like that. Bummers and letdowns. Henderson eventually went under and Costello joined Summit Sales, which was basically just Henderson reconstituted without the baneful influence of Bob Henderson, the price-fixing asshole who drove all their customers away and died of a heart attack in the men's room of the Los Angeles Convention Center, thus securing his place in industry lore. Isahakian switched firms a couple times too.

The years passing, they saw each other here and there, conventions, golf tournaments. Jack a diehard Dodgers fan. They always got along. Costello remembers telling him, at a counter day in Riverside in 1985, that he was putting in a pool. The last time Costello had money in the bank.

Then 1990, the plague. Summit went under. Costello was forty-five years old, hustling for a job, any job, making calls, pulling the girls out of Catholic school, sending them to the neighbors' for breakfast. Her minivan repossessed. Credit-card shell games. She started up an unlicensed day-care service, cash under the table, grocery money, a parade of little monsters splashing in the pool. She screamed at him at night, the kids awake across the hall. *You fucking bitch, I never took a day off in my life. Not one day.* But never out loud. Too scared of her. Just lay there, taking the blame. At one point he stopped by Home Depot and filled out an application to be a cashier. Worst day of his life. Then the call. Jack Isahakian, of the Glendale Isahakians, saying that he had nothing, absolutely nothing, because everyone was fucked at the moment, but, if Costello could stand to go back to where he'd started, he could work the order desk and maybe some days do outside stuff, straight commission work on all the dogshit wholesalers, and see what happened after that, but everyone was fucked, so no promises. Jack was a loudmouth, but a grinder, the real deal. What luck to know a good and honest man.

"Did you get the *Pipeline*?" Jack says, holding up his copy. "They cut half my quotes."

"It's still a nice little article."

"I heard from Lamrock's guy. WCPA is going all-out for the banquet this year. Prime rib, champagne, napkins."

"The decadence of Rome."

"When I win, they'll probably give me five minutes to make a speech. I'm using that gila-monster thing. It's beautiful."

Lights blaze in the outer office, marking the arrival of inside sales. Costello loads up on coffee and catalogues.

Going west on 91, against traffic. Costello, the driving virtuoso. Warehouses crowding both sides of the freeway. On each rooftop a row of spinning turbine vents. Silver spinning flowers. Costello sails over the bright and hostile neighborhoods of North Long Beach, scene of his wasted youth. The pool hall on Atlantic Avenue. During the plague, everything falling apart, he hid out there once again, a grown man, pretending he still had a job. Nine-ball at two in the afternoon. A vacation in hell. Smoke and mirrors for two months. Putting everything on the credit card. She said he looked gray, his skin was gray, and when he told her, finally, a moment of pure relief, she was there, touching his gray hand, bringing his color back.

Costello spends Monday night sitting in his chair, watching reruns of *Law & Order*. The phone rings. He never gets there in time, picks it up right when the machine turns on, creating stress and chaos for everyone involved. Gone for over a year and she's still the outgoing message. Talking over her voice, the machine beeping, the kids on the other end, annoyed.

"Dad?" one of the girls says. He can't tell their voices apart.

"Hello, hello!"

"It's Katie."

"Katie!"

"Watching the game?"

"It's a travel day. How's summer school?" She has to teach it for extra money. Teaching at a Catholic high school, a vow of poverty.

"I talked to Megan and Matt. We want to take you out on Saturday."

"Don't go to any trouble," says Costello. "You guys should enjoy your weekends."

"I'll call you Saturday."

"Okay. Well, I'll let you go."

"I don't need to be let go. I'm talking to you. We're talking."

"Okay."

"How's business?" she asks.

He tells her everything he knows about gila monsters and their lack of assholes.

"I don't think that's true," she says.

At lunch on Tuesday it's Costello vs. Luis. The warehouse crew gathering around the ping-pong table, eating pizza. Even after a few beers, Luis is nimble and cunning. A bottle of Advil rattles ceremoniously in his back pocket each time he lunges for a ball.

"Marty gets cute with the backspin," Jack warns, beer in hand. Next to him is Dave Mumbry, who took over all the dog-shit accounts after Matt left.

"How'd you get so good at ping-pong?" he asks.

"The Army," Costello says. "It's the least selective fraternity in the world."

He hears someone calling his name. Lilac perfume mingling with diesel exhaust. He turns to where Linda used to be, and then down to where she is. Linda, twenty-four years old, with a bullet in her spine.

"Five Star Pipe and Supply," she says. "Is that your guy?"

"He was Matt's, but now he's mine again."

"They ordered some brass but didn't give me a PO number."

"Ron gave me a verbal," Costello says. "I gave them ninety-day billing."

"Ninety days!" Jack shouts. "What is that, philanthropy?"

Costello follows Linda up the ramp. Doesn't know whether to help push her.

"I'll put him on a payment schedule for that stuff," she says, "but nothing else leaves the warehouse until I see some money."

"I'll take care of it," Costello says.

Later that night, Costello pulls into his driveway. There's Rocha, revving up his Harley. And Connie running out the front door, encased in denim. Down to Chili's, for a delightful evening of pillage and rape. She waves to him and off they go, her legs squeezing tight.

The house is dark and quiet. For a couple of hours, Costello sits at the dining room table, paying the bills. Still paying off the bust. Fifteen years without a vacation. Never taking her out to dinner, not once. A million Ragú dinners. But at least they never ran out of rats.

Later he turns on the TV. The Dodgers on the first night of their home stand. Down two runs in the eighth. Costello, anxious, muttering to himself, drinking straight from the two-liter bottle of Pepsi. He wanders over to the glass slider and looks out on the darkness. He turns on the pool light. A pretty shade of green and the lizard down below.

• • •

Wednesday afternoon, up in Baldwin Park, a forsaken road winding past broken cinder block, a driveway with no address, a dungeon of a warehouse, and Ron Ciavacco, proprietor of Five Star Pipe and Supply. Sitting at the counter, marking up a racing form, as Valerie, his sister and only employee, smokes and watches *Dr. Phil* on a small black-and-white. They've been going out of business for twenty-five years.

"The wolf is at the door, my friend," Costello says, and gently explains the situation. The concept of paying for goods and services. Ron, a beggar and a chooser, asks for better pricing on globe valves. They shake hands. Ron wishes him luck at the WCPA awards banquet.

"I don't care about stats," Costello says. "Just as long as we win!"

At dusk, he hides from the eastbound traffic. Drives down Cherry Avenue, passing the cemetery on his way to the beach. The strand is dull and gray. Nobody goes in the water. He walks along the bluffs, smoking, counting the tankers in the harbor, a habit since childhood. Catalina Island, a distant mirage. Sixty years in SoCal and he's never taken the boat to Catalina.

Listening to the Dodgers game on the way home. Our man from Santo Domingo dealing a shutout into the seventh inning. Gets home just in time. Big bowl of vanilla ice cream, the last two innings, and then the news. Absolutely beautiful. There's a knock at the door.

"Hi, Marty!" Francine in her bike helmet.

"Now's not a good time."

She steps inside and Costello has no choice but to set her up with a bowl of vanilla. Be thankful for small mercies,

Francine. The Nazis would've thrown you in a lime pit. Francine stares at the pictures on the bookcase, ignoring the travesty taking place right now in the top of the eighth. The manager, in his wisdom, pulling the young lefty after he gives up a walk. Let him work out of trouble, for chrissakes. Only way to become a pitcher.

"She said I could have her jewelry," Francine says.

"What?"

Francine walking down the hall, turning on the lights like she owns the place. There's no jewelry, no real jewelry, except her wedding ring. Katie has that. Francine in their bedroom, holding the rosewood jewelry box in her stubby hands.

"It's nothing fancy," Costello says. "You won't impress anyone, if that's what you're going for."

The box tucked under her arm.

"Fine. It's all yours. Come on."

Back down the hall, turning off the lights. Francine is going out the front door. She doesn't say goodbye. A Bedouin in the night.

The Dodgers closer gets lit up and they lose in extra innings. At eleven o'clock, Costello turns on the news. And then Megan calls, just to say hi. He asks her about her junior college classes and she rants and raves about the stupidity of her fellow students. She hates Orange County. Fascist this, soulless that. She wants to travel. See the watery parts of the world. She talks through the weather and into the next commercial. Sports is next. Costello starts leaning toward the side table, getting ready to hang up the phone at his first opportunity. When he sees the Dodgers highlights coming on, he says, "Well, I'll let you go."

"What are you watching?" Megan asks.

"What? Nothing."

She laughs at him. "We're taking you out Saturday, whether you like it or not."

On Thursday afternoon he drives east into the Inland Empire, alighting upon a paved, semi-incorporated nowhere called Mira Loma. Bromberg Enterprises, the Death Star, sitting in a ring of smog on the edge of the freeway, five hundred thousand square feet of blazing white concrete. Costello parks at the edge of a vast parking lot and walks a half mile through warm, gusty winds that play havoc with his hair.

Through the dark maw of loading dock #53 and into the maze. Towering rows of everything. Hundreds of warehouse crew, pushing silver gleaming hand trucks and hydraulic pallet jacks. It smells clean in here, no diesel exhaust, all the forklifts fancy and electric. A "No Smoking" sign every ten feet. At the far end a metal staircase leading to the offices of young men with advanced business degrees from accredited universities. It's only a matter of time before Bromberg swallows up Ajax and every other rep in SoCal. Death from above. Eliminate the middleman. Chris Easton, younger than Matt, but already with a wife and kids and a mortgage. A bureaucrat with class and breeding, he sits Costello down, offers him coffee, soda, popcorn, hot dogs. They've got a whole circus up here. Costello breaks down the ballcock situation. Five hundred serial numbers for five hundred faulty units, written down by hand, his own, on a yellow legal pad, plus a flow chart of rebate and compensation. The factory rep running interference for the contractor, on behalf of the contractor's wholesaler, so neither have to face the wrath of the builder. The gallant factory rep, doing his duty, meeting his challenger. Pistols at dawn.

"It's ridiculous how complicated this is," says Easton, flipping the chart upside down.

"It's what they call a Byzantine arrangement. But I've already been out on all the job sites, squared things with Lamrock. We're switching out the defectives ourselves, all you need to do is sign off on the replacements so my contractor can pull from your shelves ASAP. The purchase order numbers are already plugged in and you get the percentage on everything. You really don't have to do a goddamn thing." Calm down, calm down. "I'm just saying . . . I'm just showing you what I did so I don't have to answer questions later. It's pretty much a done deal. Our long national nightmare is over."

"Lamrock okayed this."

"Ex cathedra."

"What?"

"Lamrock okayed it."

"Can you send this to me as an Excel sheet? I can't show this mess to my boss."

"You bet. There's a gal in our office. She's dynamite with computers."

Easton laughs, like he just heard a joke, and gives back the legal pad. A new bag of Pings in the corner, a framed photograph of Easton standing next to Tiger Woods.

"Are you going to the WCPA tourney?" Costello asks.

"Harbor Municipal," he says tentatively. "That's a pretty ghetto course."

"Not if you're a hack like me."

"They should have the tournament someplace nice."

"We're lucky there's still a golf course in Southern

California that lets us play. Lamrock had to pull a lot of strings to make it happen."

"Have you actually met Lamrock?"

"If you have time," says Costello, "maybe we could go down and double-check your stock."

"It's all right here," Easton says, tapping his laptop screen. "Everything that comes in and out of here is all right here."

"I know. I just want to see it."

"Actually," says Easton, "I'm not allowed down there at the moment."

"Why not?"

"Long story."

"Oh, yeah?" Costello crosses his legs, getting comfortable. This is the job. This is the beauty of every job. Listening to stories.

"I don't have time to go into it. Just email me that sheet."

"Tell me the general area where I need to look. I'll use my Spidey sense."

"You'll get lost. I'll call somebody."

The liaison, a snaggletoothed black kid, arrives at the bottom of the stairs, driving an electric cart. Zipping down aisle 97B, a gob of tobacco under his lip.

"How come Easton stays up there?"

"Who?"

"Easton. He works upstairs."

The kid stops the cart and looks around. "A couple weeks ago, a dude got stabbed over by will call." Points ominously to a distant vector of the warehouse. "No one upstairs is allowed downstairs until the investigation is over. That side's run by Cucamonga Dogpatch. Northside Onterios are up here, running all the trim. Most of the foremen are Northside, so that's where the problem starts."

"Are you in a gang?"

"No."

"Well, Christ, be careful."

"The best part is that the guy who did it already got fired for something else."

"Does Easton know that?" Clever of young Easton, sending the old factory rep into the kill zone.

"No. We're all getting longer lunches while they do the investigation. Don't say nothing."

"I won't."

The kid gets him a mobile stair unit with suction stops. Costello spends an hour aloft, counting boxes one by one, then has a cigarette on the edge of the loading dock.

Later, driving back to Anaheim, against traffic, he pulls off to get some In-N-Out. Orders a double double animal style. Outside on the stone benches, a warm night, the sky gray and pink. Katie worked a couple summers here. Good money for fast food. Gave her acne. Or maybe it was Megan. Cute round face, both of them, like their mother. Would be nice if the kids could come to the WCPA banquet, be there when the awards are announced. But what a bummer for them, hanging around with a bunch of plumbers and toilet salesmen on a Friday night.

He stops at Home Depot and buys shock treatment for the pool. Waiting at the register. The girl trying to change the receipt, looking flustered. There but for the grace of God.

In the fading light Costello stands at the edge of the deep end. The lizard is barely visible at the bottom. He dumps in two bags' worth of calcium hypochlorite. Burns the nose. White cleansing death.

A year of radiation. A year of bedpans and vomit bowls.

Gray wispy hair like cobwebs on her head. *All so that we could have our long, precious goodbye. Pointless. It wasn't for you. I knew the young and dancing you. Disintegrating every day, pale, nauseated, dementia, that wasn't you. A thing died in our bed—it wasn't you. I should've slit your throat, babe, while you were still you.*

On Friday afternoon, before leaving the office for the tournament, Costello stops by Linda's desk and asks for help. He holds up the yellow legal pad containing all his ballcock calculations.

"Do you know how to put this in Excel?"

"Just put it there," she says, pointing to an empty spot on her desk.

"Doesn't have to be anything fancy."

She explains that she can email it to the guy at Bromberg as soon as it's done.

"Great!" Costello says. "Saves me the hassle!"

"You're late for the tournament," she says, shooing him away.

Harbor Municipal. Par-three wonderland. The parking lot full of plumbing trucks. One of them just a filthy old milk truck with no windows or decals. Instead, someone has traced "Kelly Plumbing" in the filth, along with a phone number. Blessed are the plumbers. Old guys in coveralls dragging their bags and beer coolers. Young *vato* plumbers in their Dickies, swinging wedges and putters.

Costello walks up the ninth hole. Jack and Mumbry, totally blasted, are taking practice tee shots, trying to hit a foursome who are putting on the green.

"Fuck off," one of them yells back across the fairway, his voice muffled by the sound of the 405 freeway, which is hidden behind a line of eucalyptus trees.

Jack gives the guy the finger, takes a pull on his Tecate. Mumbry points to the sand trap by the green, where a solitary figure is sprawled facedown.

"That guy passed out down there about an hour ago."

"A hundred dollars if anybody tags him from here," says Jack.

"Maybe he's dead," Costello says.

"A couple guys from Dinoffria Plumbing reported back," Mumbry says. "He's breathing."

Ajax has a tent set up. Glorious standards flapping in the wind. A few plumbers stand around drinking, looking through catalogues, playing with the new faucet models.

Mumbry has orange chicken wing sauce all around his mouth.

"You missed the Hooter girls, Marty. They were giving out hot wings."

Jack puts an arm around Dave Mumbry. "Collectively the girls opted not to fuck Dave."

"I'm a married man," says Mumbry.

"So am I," says Jack. "It's a common condition."

Costello sits down on a folding chair. A young plumber is trying to figure out the action on the new ratchet cutters. Costello steadies a piece of one-inch copper and shows him how to clamp it on.

"Is this a sample one?" the plumber asks. "Can I have it?"

"What, free?" Costello shakes his head. "Not in this life, my friend. Who's your wholesaler? I'll have him bring some in for you."

What they call pulling business through. Costello gives the kid his card.

Sirens. An ambulance rolling up the cart path. Everyone scatters as it accelerates down the fairway.

"Maybe that guy is dead," says Mumbry, but the ambulance gets halfway to the green and makes a hard left, cutting through a treeline and onto another fairway.

"When's the best ball start?" Costello asks.

"It got canceled," says Mumbry. "There's some disorganization going on."

"Then fuck it. I'm having a whack."

Costello with a nine iron. Bend the knees, let it rip. Losing the ball in the white sky, then the silence of a distant landing, four feet in front of the sand trap. Costello grabs a wedge and putter.

"If I don't return," he says, "avenge me."

The grass is summer-brown. Hot winds whirling down from the freeway. Sirocco, an old crossword word. A ball whizzes past Costello's head.

"Incoming!" Jack's voice louder than the wind. Friendly fire.

The drunk in the sand trap rolls over. Lying there, quite peaceful, with an empty bottle of peppermint schnapps next to his head, is the man himself, Lamrock, patron saint of plumbing contractors throughout the whole of Christendom.

Costello pitches his ball over the trap, over the corpus of Lamrock. The ball rolls onto the green. The flag, at first, is nowhere to be found. But then he sees it floating in the water hazard, along with several empty beer cans. Costello drops his putt, saving par.

A golf cart cresting the hill, plumbers dangling out the sides, wielding golf clubs and forty-ounce bottles of beer. A blond Hooters girl driving, swerving, laughing. She skids onto the green and someone yells, "Marty!"

Rocha, riding shotgun, has his arm over her shoulder. "Hey, neighbor! Are you loaded or what?"

"I'm just trying to get in a few whacks."

Rocha introduces his fellow technicians from Advanced Plumbing Specialists, and his young cousin, an apprentice. He introduces Mandy.

"This is crazy," she tells Costello. "Most of the shit they send us to is so boring."

"Yeah, we have a lot of fun out here," says Costello, a little too brightly, voice cracking like a thirteen-year-old. Christ, the goofiness, it never goes away.

"Marty's nominated for sales rep of the year," Rocha says, drunk, grinning ear to ear, nudging Mandy with his shoulder.

"Wow!" Mandy says, with big mocking eyes.

Just once a piece like her, just once, but never. A bit trashy, but still, a time and place for everything.

"We're speed-golfing," says Rocha. "You have to hit the ball from the cart while it's moving. It's like polo."

"The sport of kings," says Costello.

"Which hole are we on?" asks the cousin, adjusting his ponytail.

"We're going backwards numerically, I think," says Rocha. "Hey, Marty, do you know Ron Ciavacco?"

"Sure."

"He had a heart attack on fourteen."

"Is he dead?"

"No, they put him in an ambulance."

"That's good."

A cart marked "Ranger" comes over the hill. A man armed

— 218 —

with a bullhorn, yelling at everybody to go home. The WCPA Best Ball Extravaganza is drifting once more into chaos.

"Fascist motherfucker," says Rocha's little cousin.

Costello and Rocha extract Lamrock. His face plastered with drool and sand. They pour some water on him.

"It's prime rib time," says Rocha, nudging Mandy once more. "You like meat, right?"

A frozen smile. She looks trapped all of a sudden. Waiting for all of them to go away. They load Lamrock in the cart and drive up the fairway. Jack sees Lamrock and laughs.

"That was you down there? You fucking lightweight!"

"I think I got dehydrated," says Lamrock.

The Ajax standards coming down. In carts and on foot, plumbing contractors sweep across the steppes of the municipal course. The Mongol hordes. Costello helps carry the faucet displays back to the clubhouse, which is now off-limits. Through the windows the silver vats of prime rib. The wait staff taking it all back to the kitchen. Security pushing plumbers from the door.

"Somebody tell somebody that Jack Isahakian wants to eat," says Jack.

A forty-ounce shatters on the pavement. Pushing and shoving. Security on their walkie-talkies, calling in an air strike. Lamrock trying to climb in through a window. Night falling on Harbor Municipal.

"I don't think they'll let us back next year," says Mumbry.

In the end, the banquet gets held in the parking lot. The WCPA supreme council gathers everyone up and, just like that, the awards ceremony is over. Jack wins manager of the year. Mike Melendez, of Southwestern Sales, gets rep of the year. Costello congratulates Mike, who says, "That ballcock thing fucked you up."

Mike takes his trophy and leaves. Most of the guys head out, a cavalcade of plumbing trucks. Lamrock pouring shots into Dixie cups for everyone who sticks around. The lifers. The heavies. In the amber darkness, Jack mounts the hood of his Grand Marquis, holding up his plaque in triumph.

"Hey, listen up. I'm not leaving here without a speech. Somebody introduce me. No, fuck it. I'll do it myself. I'm Jack Isahakian. Some of you are lucky enough to know me." A chorus of fuck-you's. "Yeah, well, I'm a lucky man, myself. I work with a lot of highly competent professionals. Solid people, top to bottom. Warehouse, inside, outside. I can point to anyone at Ajax, man or woman, and say, 'That guy right there, he's a fucking pro.' Let me give you an example. I have five minutes, right? Most of you know Marty Costello. He's what we call a salesman. What he does is make sales calls. A couple months ago, on a rainy day, he walks in the door at Munson Pipe and Supply in Hawthorne." Some whooping and hollering from the Munson contingent. "That's what salesmen do. They show up and they walk through the door. On this day it turns out that our competition, who shall remain nameless . . . It's Gary Yeager from Carlton-Hill Sales. Is he here? I don't want to throw Gary under the bus or anything, but on this day he excused himself from walking in the door because it was raining outside. He actually called up Munson and said that. I admire his honesty, but if I felt I couldn't work because it was raining outside I wouldn't admit it to anybody. I'd go home and shoot myself. Anyway, our friends at Munson also thought it was funny, and since Marty the Brentford toilet rep was there instead of Gary the Kenner toilet rep, they thought, why not have Marty take a look at our inventory and see what's what? Forty items and ten categories later, Marty walks out of there with the biggest order of the year. And all he did was show up for work."

Jack drops his plaque. It hits the bumper on the way down and thuds on the pavement. "I had this thing planned about gila monsters, but it's getting late, comrades, and I've had a lot to drink."

A smattering of applause. Rocha and Mumbry laughing, shaking Costello's hand. The guys from Munson shaking his hand. Other wholesalers, plumbers, Lamrock.

"Somebody call Jack a cab," he says.

Saturday afternoon. The kids on their way. Costello has shocked them with an actual plan: dinner in Catalina.

But first a bit of sun. The pool turquoise. The glass slider sliding. The roof, the wall, the wires. This house is his. Or the bank's, but he still lives here.

Costello hops on the raft, pushes off, lights up. The telephone pole in the corner of the yard, like the mainmast of a ship.

He rolls off the raft and into the pure blue water. Down he goes to the bottom of the deep end. His eyes open, burning. The lizard pale from the chemicals. You never complained, not once, your hair falling out, the hideousness of your round beautiful face. That final moment, your green eyes popping open, and all the bile spilling out of you. A goddamn captain, going down with the ship.

Back on the raft, the lizard in his hand, pale and soggy, tiny black eyes and tiny white feet. Costello throws it over the wall and hears it splash in his neighbor's pool.

Acknowledgments

I want to thank the old man, Michael Gavin, and my sisters, Shannon and Kelsey. I depend on their love and support and my enduring goal in life is to make them laugh.

My agent, PJ Mark, is an ace, and I'm incredibly grateful for everyone at Simon & Schuster, especially Jonathan Karp and my wonderful editor, Anjali Singh. I want to thank Deborah Triesman at *The New Yorker* for taking a chance, and I want to thank Chuck Rosenthal and Howard Junker for their early encouragement. In 2005, I took an Extension Class at UCLA with Lou Mathews, a generous and inspiring teacher and one of the finest writers in Los Angeles. His class turned me into a writer and his continued support and friendship means the world to me. The Wallace Stegner Fellowship in Creative Writing at Stanford University gave me time to develop many of these stories and I'm very thankful for the opportunity I had to work with Tobias Wolff and Elizabeth Tallent. At Boston University I was lucky to work with Ha Jin and Allegra Goodman, and I want to give special thanks to Leslie Epstein, whose humor and commitment will always be an inspiration. Now for a long list of names. The following people have either helped me improve this book, or loaned me money: Skip Horack, Josh Tyree, Abigail Ulman, Stacey Swann, Molly Antopol, Justin St.

ACKNOWLEDGMENTS

Germain, Sarah Frisch, Stephanie Soileau, Vanessa Hutchinson, Harriet Clark, Rob Ehle, Jesmyn Ward, Will Boast, Amy Keller, Laura McKee, Josh Rivkin, Rita Mae Reese, Chanan Tigay, Mike McGriff, Emily Mitchell, Charles Donato, Stacey Mattingly, Andrew W. Euell, Laina Pruett, Jeff Howe, Antonio Elefano, Katherine Ayars, Lara Jacobs, Morgan Cotton, Dawn Dorland, Yael Schonfeld, Sarah Hinds, Jen Edwards, Mia Taylor, Chelika Yapa, Sacha Howells, Doug Knott, Krissy Klabacha, Ro Gunetilleke, Scott Doyle, Alison Turner, Ami Spishock, John Houston, Jon Rooney, Fred Schroeder, James Keane, S.J., Aric Avelino, Don Zacharias, Paul Taunton, Jeff Cox, Craig Cox, Liz Flahive, Thomas Patterson, Tim Loughran, Christin Lee, Rachel Kondo, Mary O'Malley, Mike McLaren, Tim Lugo, Adam Harris, and all the dudes at the gas station.

Finally, I want to thank Suzanne Rivecca, who is brilliant and brave and the reason I feel so lucky.

ABOUT THE AUTHOR

Jim Gavin's fiction has appeared in *The New Yorker*, *The Paris Review*, *Zoetrope*, *Slice*, and ZYZZYVA. He lives in Los Angeles.